# My Child .. Missing

## W.R. Benton

*A fictional account based on
the actual story of Jared Ropelato*

**LOOSE CANNON ENTERPRISES**
*Paradise, CA*

*2015 Edition*
*ISBN 978-1-939812-15-5*

Author Photos © Copyright 2014, by Melanie D. Calvert
© Contents Copyright 2015 by W.R. Benton
© Cover layout & design Copyright 2014 by WR Benton, LLC
Cover image of Jared by Dawn Ropelato, used with permission
Edited by: Bobbie La Cour, Daniel Williams and Kay King

www.loose-cannon.com

# Books by W.R. Benton

*My Child is Missing: Based on the True Story of Jared Ropelato*

*Alive and Alone (Young Adult)*

*The Fall of America Series*

## Non-Fiction

*Simple Survival, a Family Outdoors Guide*

*Impending Disasters*

To see more than 30 other books, ebooks and audio books
by W.R. Benton, visit:
http://www.amazon.com/author/wrbenton/

# DEDICATION

A special dedication and thanks to both Jared Ropelato and his parents, Dawn and Larry Ropelato, for allowing me to write this book. The stack of papers and comments from most of the individuals involved in Jared's rescue and his family helped me immensely. Jared is a very survival savvy young man and in the time he was missing, death could have easily visited him in the form of a mishap, hypothermia, or a dozen other dangers. Thanks to the efforts of others, both physical and in prayer, Jared was saved. While I expected this book out way before now, things beyond my control prevented that from happening. However, you are now reading it, so my goal has been reached.

To all members of our armed forces, past, present and future, for your personal and professional sacrifices while serving our great nation. May God bless each of you.

# TABLE OF CONTENTS

# FROM THE AUTHOR

While a majority of this book is pure fiction, an actual survival situation happened on August 12, 2011, vaguely similar to the way I tell this story, involving Jared Ropelato. While my story is untrue and fictional, Jared's was real and life threatening, to say the least. Can you imagine the thoughts, fears and concerns of his parents, family, and friends? As a Christian family, they turned to God, family, and friends for the safe return of their son.

You'll hear God mentioned many times in this book and I can assure you, there are very few atheists in survival situations, just like foxholes during times of war. I spent over 26 years on active duty with the United States Air Force and for a little over twelve of those years, I taught survival to air crew members. I also read hundreds of journals, or notes the USAF collected, that were written by survivors and about those who did not survive. In each reading God was mentioned often, as well as daily prayer, so all survivors turned to the belief in a higher power. If you're offended by God or religion, then I don't think this is a good book for you, but if you want an accurate account of what can happen in a survival situation, then continue reading. God is a very important player in survival, as He is in all aspects of our daily lives, but His actions are more visible when one is young, alone, cold, hungry, deeply scared, and maybe injured.

While my story of Mike is pure fiction, it is loosely based on Jared's. I have added fictitious thoughts of those involved in my great adventure, to add a clearer understanding of various events of survival. I have also changed all names involved with Mike's rescue and that was done to allow me to interject comments or actions of those assisting in the search and rescue to assist in story flow, which may or may not be accurate or even remotely like Jared's. In my story, the first part of this book, I've made no effort to reflect the true personalities of anyone associated with Jared's rescue, their thoughts, or comments, but have created my own characters, as well as plot. My plot for the fiction in this book is based loosely on Jared's but with a much wider scope, involving more action and conditions than he faced. With all of this said, keep in mind this first part is actually a work of fiction. I have lengthened it over a longer time frame and added some drama and suspense to allow for easier and more adventurous reading. I've taken full literary freedom in creating a suspenseful story and hope you enjoy it.

The search, rescue, and recovery of anyone is an emotional roller-coaster, with everyone hitting highs and lows at times, including those actually involved with the rescue. In Jared's case, he was not only very lucky, but an intelligent young man who had help from God. If not for previous Scout training and Jared's ability to stay calm in a very emotional and dangerous situation, he could very well be dead right now. Prayer aided this young man and kept him safe. Hypothermia, the lowering of the bodies core temperature, is a real killer, and that night Jared was in constant danger from this illness.

At the end of this book, I have included actual statements and comments from his parents of Jared's actual situation. Also, while the written comments of these two people may not appear accurate or seem logical to you, the reader, it all came together to save a young boy. These comments are giving credit where credit is due, but keep in mind, many others were involved that may not be mentioned at all. At the same time, it's easy to understand how Jared's parents were so concerned they forgot names or even comments made by various individuals. This is not intentional, so if your name has been left out or you're misquoted, please accept our apologies for this unintentional act. May God bless all of you for assisting the Ropelato family during their time of need and desperation. You, like Him, were there when they needed you.

Jared's parents, as well as Jared, all feel that God was with him the day he became lost and as you read the statements, you'll see certain things occurred that cannot be explained. Neither Jared's family or the author think these were coincidences, but rather they were actually God's hand in the rescue—some before it even occurred. Jared and his family are strong believers and have been since long before the survival situation, but this difficulty strengthened their beliefs, if that's possible.

So, with all of this said, I invite you to relax and enjoy my latest release, *"My Child is Missing"* based very loosely on the true survival of Jared Ropelato, with the actual story of Jared at the end of the book.

*W.R. Benton*
*Jackson, MS*

# CHAPTER 1

THE young man stopped and looked around, confused. He was sure he was on the right trail, but things looked different to him now. He pulled his ball cap off, ran his hand through his hair and thought, *If I'm lost or can't find my way back, they'll have to search and find me. I'll end up in trouble if they make a big hoopdeedo over this. I don't understand what happened, because I'm sure this is the way to camp. Maybe things just look different on the way back than they did going to the lake. I'll walk a little further.*

As Mike walked, he didn't notice the dark clouds moving low overhead or which direction he was going. While young, he was only eleven, he didn't expect any problems on his way back to get more fishing lures; after all, he was a Boy Scout. He'd been fishing, snagged his last lure, and needed more. He didn't figure he'd be gone long enough for anyone to miss him, so he'd told no one he was leaving the group. *I think not bringing someone with me, like an adult, was a big mistake,* he thought, and scanned the countryside as he moved.

There came a loud *boom* of thunder and the young man looked up at the swirling dark sky. The clouds were rolling and moving quickly from the western horizon. *Not good for me,* he thought and then wondered, *should I make a shelter or keep walking? I need a shelter of some kind, because while it's warm, I think hypothermia could be a problem. It's a good thing Scouts taught me all of this stuff.*

Moving to a huge pine tree, he cut a few of the lower limbs off and moved under the long branches that extended in varying lengths from the trunk.  He knew the tree would only protect him from a light to moderate rain and in a downpour, he'd get soaked. *This will have to be good enough for now.  I think I'm lost and as soon as the storm stops, I'll move back the way I came.  I just hope I can remember which direction I went at the forks in the trail.*

Mike moved closer to the tree, heard the rain drops striking the branches, and could see rain falling in the distance.  He was scared now, not so much from the weather, it was just rain, but with the knowledge he might be in trouble.  He felt he could spend the night and while it'd not be comfortable, he wouldn't die, or would he?  What concerned him was the decisions he had to make and knowing the wrong one could lead to a big mess. The last thing he wanted was search teams looking for him and making him look a little kid. *Mom and dad will be worried at first, but they'll raise a fuss if folks have to look for me,* he thought and then pulled his backpack off. He placed it on the ground beside him.

Suddenly, pulling the pack to him, he placed it between his legs and opened it. *I need to see what I have and don't have, just in case I have to spend the night,* he thought.

Unknowingly, he began to speak aloud, "Another pair of hiking shorts, change of socks, some waterproof matches, collapsible cup, one chocolate bar, small bag of trail mix, peanut butter sandwich for lunch, a small pocket knife, and some coins. At the very bottom he discovered a poncho. "Not much to eat here." He removed the poncho.

In the back of his mind, he remembered his Scout Master saying, "While most of you will be concerned about food in a survival situation, your biggest need is water.  Even in mild weather, the loss of water can kill you after a few days have lapsed.  Also, hypothermia is another issue to constantly think about.  The lowering of the bodies core temperature can kill, even if the temperature is as high as in the 70's.  Say you fall into a spring fed stream, which we all know is cold;

hypothermia could result if the air temperature is low enough."

*What else did he say?* Mike thought and his mind began to remember, "Your first step is to make a shelter, fire, and collect water."

*Not yet. I don't even know if I'm lost yet. I do know if I'm not back by dark, they'll be forced to call the police or whoever they call when someone is lost,* he thought and then glanced at the dark sky as he prayed, "Lord, I'm Mike and you know me. I've never asked you for much, unless a family member is sick, in trouble, or dying, but I need your help today. I need you to guide my feet later, when I walk away from here, and help me find my way back to camp. I don't want to worry people and if you decide I should stay out here, then help me survive. I learned in church that all things are possible through you, so I'm asking you to save me."

He thought for a second, could not think of anything else to say so he closed his prayer with, "This I ask in the name of Jesus, amen."

His spirits were lifted by the simple prayer, but he knew he was still in a serious situation. As he sat there thinking, he suddenly noticed his breath coming from his mouth like smoke. *The temperature has dropped a great deal since earlier, he thought and then wondered, should I make a fire? If I make one, it'll have to be small, because the limbs on this tree are too low. I can't cut them off, because my knife blade is too small.*

He knew how to make a fire and had earned merit badges in fire safety, camping, and wilderness survival. He had many more badges, but these were the ones he needed most right now. He broke dead limbs from the Pine he was under and then moved out into the rain to collect more wood. Once he had a large pile, he pulled his knife and shaved some long pieces of wood to start his fire. *I have tinder, kindling, and fuel,* he thought with a grin. *I have all I need.*

Striking his first match, the wind blew it out before he could lower the flame to his wood. He moved, had his back to the wind and struck another match. The match head ignited and within seconds the tinder was burning. He then slowly added larger pieces of kindling to his flames. After a few minutes, he placed a much larger, but yet small log on the minute fire. It was about the size of one of his momma's cup saucers, but big enough he felt the heat. *I can't let this get out of control or I'll start a forest fire and burn myself to death. Keep it small, keep an eye on it, and feed it, so it doesn't go out,* he though as he pulled the peanut butter sandwich from his pack. He tore it in half, saving the other half for tomorrow.

Taking a big bite, he thought, *I'll be grounded until I'm thirty years old. I don't see how I missed the trail. Mom and dad will be so upset with me.* He felt a strong gust of wind and the flames of his fire flickered and danced. *Getting pretty cold out there now.*

It was at this point he noticed ice forming on the lowest limb of his crude shelter. *Whoa, ice; so the temperature must be below freezing and me without a sleeping bag or blanket. I won't freeze to death, not if I stay beside my fire, but I'll have to stay awake all night and feed my flames. If the fire goes out, I'm dead. It's starting to grow dark too. If I get too cold, I can dig a hole in the dirt and cover myself with dead leaves to keep me warm.*

An hour later, stiff from sitting in one position, he glanced toward the sky and saw sleet falling. It was then he heard it striking his tree. He re-positioned his rear and then sat Indian style beside his flickering flames. Darkness soon arrived and it found him still under the pine.

The hours passed slowly for Mike as he grew chilled and fed his flames. At one point, he was tempted to eat the other half of his sandwich, but quickly decided that wouldn't be smart. While his stomach growled and made noises, he knew he wasn't close to starving. He did miss home, where he could walk to the fridge open the door and find something to eat. Or, open a cupboard and pull out a snack or drink.

Near midnight, with the temperature near or below freezing, he increased the size of his fire slightly, because he was getting cold. Sleet was still falling and the earlier rain had frozen to the limbs on his tree. Standing, he saw about a quarter of an inch of ice on his tree. He was starting to shake from the frigid air, which he knew was the first sign of hypothermia. He was dressed in a long sleeve shirt, pair of shorts, long socks and boots. It was then he remembered the poncho, so he pulled it on, hoping it would help him retain some body heat. After wearing the poncho for a few minutes he discovered it worked and he was getting warmer.

*I read someplace that I need to keep the neck open to allow my sweat to leave or I'll get wet under the poncho,* he thought as he unknowingly smiled. For the first time since darkness, he was fairly warm. *Thank you, Lord, for allowing me to remember my poncho!*

As he warmed, the young man grew sleepy and it was hours after midnight when he closed his tired eyes, intending to only rest them for a few minutes, and his head slowly lowered to his chest. Seconds later, Mike was asleep.

A couple of hours before daylight, Mike woke feeling deeply chilled. At first he was confused and wondering why he was in the woods, but then remembered. Glancing at his almost dead fire, he was suddenly filled with fear. All that remained were a few red coals. He added a few dry sticks on the coals and blew on them gently. It didn't work, so he re-positioned the sticks and blew again, and this time they flared up nicely. He soon had his fire burning once more. The earlier sleet had turned to a light snow and while not deep, the whole area around him was covered in virgin white.

*While it's beautiful,* he thought, *it'll make it harder on anyone looking for me. Lord, don't let anyone searching fall or slip and break a leg. I already feel bad enough that I got lost; if someone gets hurt or killed while looking for me, I don't think I could take that happening. How did I fall asleep? I remember resting my eyes and then nothing. That's pretty stupid and could get me killed and it'd all be my fault. Today, once the sun comes up, I need to make a better shelter.*

He'd just added a small log to his fire when he heard the lonely cry of a wolf, or maybe it was a coyote, because he was unsure. It was loud and filled him instantly with a deep feeling of home sickness and fear. Tears began to fall as he thought, *I don't have time to cry, so I need to stop this. I want to go home, but that won't happen until someone finds me. Babies cry and while I want everyone to treat me like a grownup, I'm acting like a child. Stop it now!*

He wiped his eyes with the back of his hand, but continued to sniffle. He realized for the first time in his young life he was truly alone and only he could keep himself alive. In the past his parents or other adults had cared for him and he'd lived a comfortable life. Now, he was hunkered down by a small fire, wearing a poncho, and not even able to sleep or his fire would go out. He was bone aching tired, needed a bath, and a night of full sleep, but there was nothing he could do right now about any of his problems. This, he realized as he shook his head, was his first chance to behave as a real adult and he wasn't sure he was up to the task.

*Stop feeling sorry for yourself and be glad to be alive,* he thought and tried to smile. It was hard, but he'd learned about the will to survive when he'd earned his merit badge in wilderness survival. Folks that really wanted to live didn't give up and most were found alive, while those who gave up, usually were found dead. Mike wanted to live more than anything at this moment, and decided he'd keep working to survive and do what it took to return home safely. He knew others had survived and in more dangerous situations than his.

When he'd earned his merit badge in rescue and recovery, he'd learned that most rescues happened within the first 48 hours a person was missing. As near as he could tell, he'd been gone for almost 12 hours, so it wasn't likely anyone was really out in the cold looking for him yet. He knew teams would need to be formed, a control center established, and it all had to be coordinated by one centralized rescue center. It wasn't just a mob of people moving all over the mountains looking for a person. The map was marked off in sections and one-at-a-time they were combed for any sign of the missing person. They'd start near the lake where he'd been fishing and then slowly move outward.

*Lord, he prayed silently, give my parents strength. I know mom will freak out and be terrified when told I'm missing. Dad will be worried, but I think he'll handle it better because he's an assistant Scout leader. He knows I've earned a lot of merit badges, so he knows I've had training. No matter what happens, God, I do want to be rescued, but thy will be done, amen.*

Daylight was still cold and spitting sleet, now mixed with snow. The wind picked up and ice could be heard cracking as the limbs swayed, some violently. Mike was still semi-warm, but knew over the course of a day he'd get cold, even with a fire. He needed a real shelter and the sooner the better.

He thought of the various shelters he'd seen in survival manuals, and all required material to cover a wooden frame. *I don't have anything to cover a frame with, so I will have to use limbs and tree branches. Pine boughs will work, but I'll have to break them off,* he thought as he stood and looked the trees over closely.

He added some small pieces of wood to his fire, but not too much, in case the wind grew worse; he didn't want to catch the tree on fire. His biggest fear was returning and finding his fire was out. While he still had matches, a fire would be much harder to light now, since he'd burned up most of his dry wood and the wind was howling.

Bending over, he pulled his socks up as high as he could, pulled the belt from his shorts and placed it around his poncho, to keep it snug against him and to fight the loss of body heat. He stepped from the warmth of the shelter and moved into the wind.

He decided almost immediately making a shelter in this wind would be impossible, so he moved from tree to tree, gathering firewood. *I'll have to wait where I am until the wind dies down before I can even consider a new shelter.*

Back under the tree shelter, he placed some wood on his fire and pulled the chocolate bar from his pack. It was formed as one large bar, made up of smaller pieces that could be broken off and eaten. He removed two squares and said, "Thank you Lord for the food I'm about to receive. I know it is less than you normally provide me, but it is enough. I ask you, God, to send help to me, so I can return home and become a better person. I will promise you nothing, except I will try to be a better person and no longer complain when I have to get up to go to church. This I ask in the name of Jesus, amen."

Over morning the wind died down and Mike knew he needed to move. He needed to be closer to water and as far as he knew, none was close to him. *I'll move downhill, because my Scout Master said streams also move downhill and eventually, I'll find water. Now, it may be a stream, lake or pond, but it'll be water,* he thought as he put his fire out.

Putting his pack on, he started down the trail, having completely forgotten about moving back up his trail. Mike was cold, famished, and tired. The lack of sleep was hard on him and he was known to sleep for long periods of time at home. Last night, he might have slept two hours. His usual sharp mind was fatigued and his thinking was slow.

As he moved, his eyes felt like they had sand in them and his body was so tired. His back was sore from sleeping and sitting up all night, along with his neck being stiff. He staggered, like a drunken man he'd once seen in town, as he moved over the mountainside. He grew concerned when he began to fall and stumble. At one point, he fell to the trail and rolled down a slight incline before he stopped. Mike, however, didn't stop, because he knew he had to have water to survive and water he'd have before he quit moving.

By midday, he'd still not found water, and he decided to avoid eating anything for lunch. *I'll save what I have for supper later,* he thought.

He heard thunder and glancing up, he saw dark clouds forming. At one point he saw a plane, but it was way too high in the air to be looking for him. It was just a small dot in the sky, leaving contrails, as it flew to some unknown destination.

It was close to three by his watch before he came to a small babbling brook that ran from the face of the mountain and followed the contours down a ravine to the valley somewhere below. He stopped, looked at the sky and saw the clouds were still overhead. Next, he laid out flat beside the stream and took a few deep drinks of water. He knew the water needed purifying and then he remembered his folding cup. It was aluminum and he wasn't sure if he could boil water in it without melting it. It's lightweight so the heat of an open flame might melt it. *It was dumb to drink this water, so I need to get a shelter up, make a fire, and then see if I can boil water in my cup. I'm not sure how high up I am. I seem to remember something about boiling the water a minute for each one thousand feet of altitude, I think is what I heard,* he thought as he moved into the trees looking for two trees, side-by-side.

His shelter would be a simple lean-to, using pine boughs for the roof and sides. He also planned to line the floor with boughs to keep him off the cold ground and to insulate his floor. Once his shelter was up, he'd make a wind block near where he'd have his fire and there were plenty of dead logs around that could be used.

Snakes never entered Mike's head as he moved through the woods gathering wood. He knew there were snakes in the area, but with the weather turning cold suddenly, serpents were the last thing on his mind. He figured they'd gone wherever snakes go when the weather turned nasty and cold.

He'd gathered up almost a full load of wood, when he reached down to get one last piece. He heard a rattlesnake's telltale rattle, felt something hit his right hand, and then looking toward the noise, he spotted a big timber rattler. The snake was only about two feet away, out in the warm sun, and Mike dropped his wood. The snake's tongue was moving in and out of its mouth, and its head followed the young man's every movement.

He glanced at his hand and saw two small puncture wounds and blood was flowing freely from each. Frightened of the snake, he picked up a stick from his gathered wood and killed it with repeated blows to the head. It was after the snake was dead that his pain started. Knowing he needed the wood or he'd eventually freeze to death, he gathered it up again and made his way back to camp.

By the time he sat by his small fire, his hand was swelling and his pain grew severe. Glancing up at the scattered clouds, he prayed aloud, "Lord, help me through this, because I'm scared to death. I need medical help, but I'm alone. I need you to help kill the pain, God, and to heal me. Amen."

Seeing his hand was still bleeding, Mike pulled his pack to him and removed a pair of socks. Using his knife, he cut a clean sock in strips to dress his injury. He knew the puncture wounds would not cause him to bleed to death nor were they much of an injury. His danger, as he knew well, was from the snake venom now in his system. His whole arm now throbbed in pain and was already swollen to twice it's normal size.

Mike tried to remember all he could about snakebites, but he knew little to start with and his panic was making thinking difficult. He knew in the old days they used to cut an "X" over each fang mark and then attempted to suck the poison out. The last he'd read, a doctor did not recommend cutting the injury because it just increased tissue damage, and sucking the poison out wasn't a good idea either.

He'd read in an old military survival manual when he was working on his merit badges that less than one percent of the people bitten by pit vipers would die without any treatment, as long as they were healthy and in good physical shape. As far as Mike was concerned, he was healthy and had just passed a football physical by the family doctor.

*I need to slow my thinking down and try to rest. Maybe if I can sleep or just chill out a while the swelling will go down. I still have no idea where I'm at, but I have sources for food and water. I read once that a person can live for weeks as long as they have water. I have that, but I sure hope it doesn't take weeks for me to be found. Right now I hurt, oh, do I hurt, but I don't think I'm in danger of dying. Doctor Myers said I was a healthy young man and I'm sure if he'd found anything wrong he would have told mom and dad.*

*Oh, I hurt,* he thought as he leaned back to the pine boughs in his shelter. He was so tired, from being up most of the night feeding his fire, that he soon fell asleep. As he slept, his arm continued to swell as the poison moved through his system.

# CHAPTER 2

TWO hours passed at the lake before Scout Billy Wilson, called 'Catfish' by all the others, asked, "Has anyone seen Mike? The last I heard, he was returning to camp for more lures." He was called by the nickname because he loved to fish for catfish.

Timmy Crawford pulled his cap off, scratched his head and said, "No, not me. The last time I saw him was hours ago." Tim was tall and lanky and wore his glasses low on his thin nose.

Ira Banks, fishing between the two asked, "When did he leave here and why weren't we told?"

"Mr. Banks, he's been gone a long time and he was just going back to camp for lures. Didn't he tell you he was leaving?"

Shaking his head, Ira said, "No, not a word."

"I saw 'em leave and he was headed back properly." Scout Giles Carter said as he moved toward the assistant Scout Leader. Giles was a quiet young man, who would rather listen than speak. He lived on a ranch.

Turning, Ira called out, "Frank, did Mike tell you he was heading back to camp earlier?"

"No," Frank Bailey replied and started walking toward the group, "but it's likely he returned and fell asleep or something."

Catfish said, "I don't think so, Mr. Bailey, because the fish are hitting and Mike loves to fish."

There came a bright light across the sky and a loud *crack* of thunder, followed by a gentle wind from the west. Rain began to fall moments later. The two Scout Leaders were professional men who volunteered their time to teach young men about scouting, and of average height and weight. While Bailey had auburn hair and Banks had black, they wore it short. Each was intelligent, with years of scouting experience, and Banks had made Eagle Scout in his younger days. Bailey had been a Sergeant in the military, so they were well qualified to lead the boys, both in and out of the woods.

*Dang, I hope the boy is in his tent. This is not the best weather to be out looking for someone.*

*If he's not at camp, I'll have to notify the police, because this is some rough country,* Bailey thought, but said, "Let's all return to camp and when we get there, I need to speak with Mike privately. He knew he was to tell Ira or me he was leaving."

"Mr. Bailey, I don't think Mike meant to do anything wrong. He asked me if I had any lures and I told him to get his own. Right after that, I saw him leaving." Scout Giles Carter said. Giles was carrying a few extra pounds and while he liked scouting, he wasn't crazy about the outdoors. He was more interested in his computer, games, or other electronic toys.

"Well, nonetheless, when we return, Mike and I will have our talk. The rules must be obeyed by everyone or there is no reason to have them. Now, let's all return to camp and get out of this rain."

The walk back was pretty much uneventful, except Catfish slipped and fell to his butt in the mud. He'd handled it well and even took the joking in a good manner. He, like everyone else, hoped they'd see Mike's smiling face at his tent, but that was not to be.

Five minutes after arriving, Frank said, "He's not here and it looks as if he's not been back. I see nothing missing and his stuff is all neatly packed away, just like the other boys. We have a problem on our hands."

"Relax a few minutes, because he might have gone to the latrine or for water."

"Ira, why would he go for water when we have two five gallon containers in our tent? As for using the latrine in this rain, I don't think so. However, Timmy, run to the latrine and see if Mike is there."

Less than five minutes later, Timmy returned, shook his head and said, "No, he's not there and it doesn't look any different than it did this morning. I'm getting scared now."

Ira said, "You guys go into your tents and change into some dry clothing." Looking at Frank, he then nodded toward the tent they shared.

*****

Mrs. Wendy Nash was looking out the window of her kitchen; it was raining harder now, and she saw a state trooper enter their long gravel driveway. They lived on a large plot of land that belonged to her father before his death, but it was hers now. *Lord, please let Mike and the other boys be safe,* she thought as she moved toward the porch.

Trooper John Michaels got out of his car and walked to the porch where he asked, "Evening Wendy, is Peter at home?"

"Hello, John, no, he's out in the fields. Is everything alright?"

"Can you call him in? I have something to tell you and I'd rather only have to say this once."

*Oh, my God, no! Please, God, let the boys all be safe,* she thought and then said, "Y . . . yes, he has his cell phone."

"Call him and I'll let you know what I know at this point."

Wendy's hands were shaking as she called her husband and then said, "He'll be right here. John, are the boys all okay?"

John met her eyes and replied, "Mike is missing, but we have reason to think he wandered off the trail and became lost. The other boys are fine, but remember, your son is a scout."

Wendy moved to the sofa and sat down, her mind filled with so many questions that she felt overloaded. *This can't be happening. How did he disappear while with the other boys? Does he have food? Water?*

*I hate this part of my job,* Trooper Michaels thought and then he said, "Wendy, we have no reason to suspect anything has happened to Mike. Kids get lost every day in the woods and usually it's because they get turned around."

Peter drove up, jumped from his field truck and made his way inside. He saw the worried look on Wendy's face and asked, "Has something happened to Mike?"

Trooper Michaels said, "He's lost is all we know right now, Pete. If you want, you can go to the mobile command post we have on the mountain. Our trailer is there as we organize and you're both welcome."

"On Baldy?" Pete asked.

"Yep, at the base of the mountain, near the visitor's center."

Wendy stood as Peter said, "You go on, John, we'll be up in a few minutes. We have to secure this place before we can leave. Do we need to bring anything?"

"No, we'll have everything you'll need, but dress warmly. And, Pete, like Pastor Fortner said last Sunday in church, 'Everything in life, every little detail, happens because God wants it to happen. It happens for a reason.' So, remember that sermon. We'll find Mike, but it might take us a while."

\*\*\*\*\*

The ride to the mountain took forever in Wendy's mind, and she actually felt she could get out and run faster than the truck, but knew better. The mountain was close to fifty miles and it was good road, until they turned off the main road and started toward the peak. Then, it was gravel and Peter had to keep his speed down to be safe.

"Thirty is tops on this road, baby, because the last thing we need now is an accident when our son needs us."

"I'm so worried. He's too young to spend the night alone in the woods."

"I won't argue with you, because I'm worried too, but Mike knows the woods better than most adults. If anyone can survive, our boy can do the job."

"He is eleven years old, Pete! You make him sound like he's some mountain man or something." Wendy shot back and immediately wanted to recall her words.

He knew she was scared, but he'd meant what he'd told her. He smiled and said, "Baby, I know you're scared and so am I, but he really is good in the woods. He's been camping since the first grade and in scouts from about the same time. He has all kinds of Merit Badges and he really knows his way around in the woods. Relax, he probably took a wrong trail and is lost. I'll bet this time tomorrow we'll all three be home laughing about this whole mess."

"I know he's good outdoors, but he's my baby and to think he's all alone on the side of this mountains worries me."

"We have a reason to be worried, but let's stay out of the way and let the professionals do their jobs. I know, as a woman and mother, it'll be hard on you, but Mike is my son too, so remember this." He grabbed Wendy's hand and gave it a gentle squeeze, which she returned.

Ten minutes later, they pulled into the parking lot of the visitor's center and Peter pulled into an empty spot. A huge mobile home, with Emergency Rescue and Recovery on the side, sat near the main building. Men and women were seen coming and going from the rescue center. Peter noticed a satellite dish on top and pointed it out to Wendy.

"They've got good communications and all kinds of stuff to help in a rescue."

"Maybe. I just want Mike back safe and sound."

Trooper Michaels waved to them and the called out, "Come on in the trailer and I'll introduce you to the folks running this thing."

When they entered, the Trooper asked, "Coffee?"

"No. No, thank you." Said Wendy, feeling her apprehension building.

"Black." Peter replied.

A tall muscular man wearing a military camouflage utility uniform neared and said, "I'm Captain John W. Smith and I'm in charge of the search and rescue unit." He extended his hand and as they shook he added, "We think Mike took a wrong trail and I currently have men and women on ATV's searching for him. What concerns me is the temperature on the mountain is just slightly above freezing, so hypothermia is a real concern for your son. Come with me to the map and I'll show you the problem we're facing."

A large topographical map was pinned to a wall and while it meant little to Wendy, Peter knew how to read it from his hitch in the army.

"Now, as you can both see, the mountain is a maze of trails, which split off into other trails, which split into other trails. I have my folks working the main trails now, looking for Mike, any sign of his passing, or anything he may have dropped or thrown away. If we find nothing on the main trails, we'll start looking on the secondary trails. Now, in the morning, once the weather clears, I have a couple of choppers coming in and even some cowboys from a couple of ranches to help. Now, the cowboys hunt this area and they'll be a great help."

"It'll be dark in a couple of hours," Wendy said, "will your people return here?"

"No, as cold as it is we think Mike will have a fire. We do know all the Scouts carried matches and lunches, so it's not likely your son will freeze or starve to death before daylight. If he's smart, he's moved toward water."

"Why?" Wendy asked.

"When most folks think of survival, they think of food and hunger. Mike has been trained in survival, so he'll know water is his greatest need. We know he has an aluminum cup, a candy bar, and extra socks and another pair of hiking shorts."

"What kinds of wild animals are in the area?" Peter asked.

"Well, there are bear, deer, porcupines, bobcats, snakes, and other small game. Folks talk about wolves being here, but the Park Rangers have never seen one."

"Bears?" Wendy asked and then continued, "But, won't they be asleep with winter coming on?"

"No, not yet. They won't go into hibernation for another month. I'd be more worried about hypothermia or snakes than a bear."

"Will snakes be out in the cold like this?"

"No, but they'll crawl out as soon as this front moves on and the sun comes out. See, they love to sun in warm weather."

Peter thought for a minute and then asked, "What kinds of snakes are on this mountainside?"

"A bunch of different kinds. Two types of rattlesnakes, which are really the only snake we're worried about. Now, they'll cause a great deal of pain, but it's unheard of for a healthy person to die, even if untreated, from a bite by a pit viper. But, if they're bitten on the neck or if they're real old or young, they might die."

"Back to the bears." Wendy said and then asked, "What are the chances of him running into one?"

"I don't really know. However, I did speak with Tom Pittman, the scout and tracker I have, and he said it would be extremely rare. Bears usually shy away from the scent of man."

"But, it could happen?"

"Yep, but he could be struck by lightning too, Mrs. Nash, so figure the odds. We don't play the *what if game* in rescue. We do things by the book and we'll find your son, except maybe not as fast as you'd like."

"I'm just worried about my son." Wendy replied.

"Your son has been trained and while he's no survival expert, he does know enough to get a shelter up, collect water, and make a fire. Those steps alone will keep him alive. Now, toward the front of the trailer, you'll find two sofas; go have a seat and if anything new comes up, I'll let you know."

Hours passed slowly, with men and women coming and going. As they waited, friends and family arrived, all praying for Mike's safety.

The rain turned to sleet and ice covered the trailer, as well as the trees and ground. They'd all moved outside to stretch their legs and get a breath of fresh air when the sleet was first noticed.

"Oh no," Wendy said, her fear obvious, "it's sleeting! Can Mike survive in weather like this?"

"If he has a shelter and fire, he'll be fine. It'll be cold, because it's cold enough to freeze, but pray this doesn't turn to snow. He can survive the snow too, but it'll be really rough on him. Keep in mind, he's wearing a pair of hiking shorts and has another pair in his pack. He's not dressed well, not for this change in weather, but a shelter and fire will save his life."

An unknown man walked to the group and asked, "Do any of you know where I can find Peter and Wendy Nash?"

"I'm Peter and this is my wife, Wendy." He nodded toward her.

Extending his hand, the man said, "I'm Major Henry Bolin, Civil Air Patrol pilot and I'll be looking for your son in the morning. I'll have my spotter, Sergeant James Calvert, with me as we search for your son."

As they shook, Peter asked, "Any idea where my son might be on this mountain?"

"It's hard to say really. Kids and older folks tend to move around a great deal, hoping to make it out on their own. Most of the time they do this because they expect to be in trouble if lost, and it only makes it harder for search teams. When a person first realizes they're lost, which can happen to the most experienced of people, they should park their rears and stay right there, if they have water and wood for a fire."

"So, you really have no idea where he could be right now?"

"No, we have no idea at this moment. See, the more they move, the more lost they get. It's like looking for someone in a shopping mall. If you continue to look for them, it may take you hours to find them, if ever. But, if you locate a bench and sit down, they'll eventually walk by you. Now, in Mike's case, we need to find him, but that'll not happen easily, not as long as he's moving."

"How do you expect to find him?" Wendy asked and then added, "I mean even if he's sitting in one spot?"

"Often we see the smoke from fires, especially after a hard rain, snow or sleet, which makes the wood wet. Wet wood smokes. Or, at night we can see his fire and as long as he stays in that spot, we simply mark our map and then send a ground team to him the next morning. There is a lot of experience here and on the mountain right now looking for your son, and we'll do our best to find him."

Peter said, "I want to thank all of you for your help. It's hard when someone you love is in danger or lost, especially a young member of our family."

"You're very welcome for our searching, because that's what most of us do as volunteers, and often we have military backgrounds in search and rescue. I flew search and rescue in the Air Force for over 20 years and have a lot of experience. Joshua Boozer, who you don't know yet, is a retired PJ, or Parachute Jumper, with hundreds of saves under his belt. He and my spotter will be here a couple of hours before dawn. Sergeant Calvert is a good spotter with an associate degree from the Community College of the Air Force in search and rescue survival operations. Every man or woman on this team was selected because of their education and experience. We'll find Mike, but it might take us some time."

"Then," Wendy lowered her head, "the problem may be if you find him alive or, uh, dead, right?"

"Most survivors in the states are rescued within 48 hours of being reported lost. We have a very high rescue rate and yes, to be completely honest, Mike has to survive long enough for us to get to him. But, I understand he's a smart young man, so I have confidence in him."

"He's just a child." Wendy blurted out and immediately felt she'd said the wrong words.

"Legally he's a child, but don't cut the boy short. He has Merit Badges in everything that will help him stay alive. I'd be real surprised if we find him and he's in danger. He *knows* what to do, so all he has to do is what needs to be done."

"I'm sorry if I sound so negative, but I love him." Wendy said and then burst into tears.

Her brother, Thomas Armstrong, pulled her near and she lowered her head to his wide shoulders. He handed her a handkerchief from his rear pocket and said, "No more talk of death. Mike is a tough kid and has Armstrong blood in him, so he's no quitter."

"But, he might be hurt or dead."

"Yep, he might be," Thomas said, "but until they carry his body off the side of this mountain, I'll not give up on him. You need to toughen up sis, because this will be an emotional roller-coaster for all of us and I want us to try and keep our attitudes positive."

"I . . . I'll try, but it's hard, Tom."

"Pray, sis, because he needs the good Lord's help, and it'll make you feel better."

Wendy nodded, but didn't reply. While she made no noise, tears ran down her cheeks.

Peter was torn apart emotionally, but knew having the family around gave both of them support. He'd been praying and would continue to pray until Mike returned. He'd always enjoyed a closeness with God and with Mike missing, he felt even closer. He knew there was a reason for his son to be where he was and if God wanted Peter to know why, he'd be shown later. For tonight, he was comforted by the simple fact he'd prayed, and knew God heard him.

Thomas, always strong spiritually, suddenly suggested, "Shall we pray?"

They were standing near a small campfire with sleet falling as they started holding hands, and when Peter extended his hand, Major Bolin took it and gave him a squeeze. Peter felt right then, as Thomas prayed for the safe return of Mike, that the right people were searching for his son.

# CHAPTER 3

TWO hours before dawn, a large group gathered in front of the trailer, most holding cups of steaming coffee or tea in their hands. It was cold, below freezing, and Peter knew the mountain passes were even colder. A light wind blew and the sleet had stopped, but the temperature had gone down. As he stood, amazed at the number of people who'd volunteered their time to look for Mike, he could see his breath each time he exhaled. *Lord,* he thought, *keep my son warm this cold morning.*

John Smith walked from the trailer and said, "I need to see the leaders of teams on foot, riding ATV's, or horses. The rest of you move to the warmth of the fires and wait. Leaders, please join me inside so we can go over the map. Peter and Wendy, if you would, please join us."

Once inside, Smith turned to a woman sitting by a stack of electronics and said, "This is Barbara Adams, our radio operator and she really runs things around here. She keeps me around to answer the phone."

Everyone laughed and then Peter and Wendy shook her hand.

Smith moved to the large map and said, "Please, I need everyone to move close to the map and pay close attention."

The laughing died and everyone moved to the map.

"This is the lake," Smith said as he pointed to the water on the map, "and we suspect that Mike started down one of these three trails initially. It's likely, at some point, he moved onto another trail. If he is like most survivors he took the easiest route, which means he's moving downhill." As he'd spoken, his hands moved along the trails on the map.

"So," Fred Bradley, a local rancher asked, "how do you want us to search?"

"In grids, or sections first. I'll assign those to each of you in a few minutes. We'll start at the lake and slowly expand out and down the mountain. Each of you will be given a radio, but don't contact us unless it's something important. We don't want useless chatter on the radio, so when he's found we'll hear it, and then can get him out. Any questions?"

The men looked determined, but no one had any questions.

Smith then discussed the various grids each group would search and finally sent the men out to start. Off in the valleys below, Peter could see low gray clouds hanging like a veil over the land. He prayed once more.

\*\*\*\*\*

Silas Hall, another rancher, sat on his horse beside Fred Bradley and said, "With the sleet from last night and high winds, it's not likely we'll find the boy's tracks."

"Silas, we have to look or do you want to go back and tell his momma we won't try? I'll not do that, old son, because she looked rough enough this morning, which means she likely cried all night. I'm a mean old coot with men, but I'm a pussycat around women."

"No," Silas said with a grin, "you misunderstood what I meant. I was just statin' the facts. I don't reckon this boy will be any harder to find than a cougar, and we've both hunted them."

"The big difference is, this young man is someone's baby boy, even if he is almost a man."

"Ben, get the riders spaced out and let's start our search!" Silas yelled to his ramrod and then yelled, "Oliver, you stay with the boys."

Fred laughed and then said, "That girl of yours is something special, my friend, and I'm willing to bet, she'll marry an extraordinary man one day."

Silas laughed, slapped his right knee and said, "It'd take an exceptional man to marry up with Oliver, because she's as rough as the boys. I'll admit, most of it is my fault and I should have found me a woman after Pearl died, but God didn't send one into my life." He then tapped his horse into a slow walk.

"Pard, she's all woman on the inside and has all them bumps and curves a woman is supposed to have, so she'll make out fine. Besides, she's a regular church goin' woman and they're hard to find these days. Don't worry about her getting muddy and bein' rough, because most tomboys make a rancher or cowboy a good wife. Just let her be and let God handle it in the future."

Hours passed with nothing seen, but suddenly, Oliver yelled out, "I got something over here!"

The group rode to her and all dismounted.

"Y'all stay by your horses. The last thing Silas and I need is for all the sign to be tracked up." Fred said and then, with Hall at his side, they moved to the remains of a small fire, under a large tree.

"He's smart for a lad," Silas said, "he used the branches of the tree for a shelter and kept his fire small. Now, I think this young man is a thinker and that'll help keep him alive."

"I don't see any blood or any sign of him being injured, do you?"

"No, and I was lookin' too. My biggest fear is his body might get too cold and then it's all over."

"He knows that too. Notice how his shelter is taking most of the wind and his fire is downwind? I'm willin' to bet he knows all about the chills and body temperature. Heck fire, I'd not be surprised if this boy didn't welcome us to his camp with a meal cookin' on a spit."

They all shared a laugh and then Fred pulled his map and checked the coordinates. Picking up the hand-held radio his said, "Rescue Base, Cowboy 1, over."

"Go ahead, Cowboy."

"Rescue Base, we found the fresh remains of an emergency shelter and fire, but no physical sign of the Nash boy. He's survival smart and while it could be the remains of another camper, I doubt it." Fred gave the map information and then added, "We'll continue downhill from here."

"Copy, Cowboy, and good luck."

"All right, now everyone take a look around and see if we missed anything." Silas ordered.

After about twenty minutes, Fred said, "Mount up, we're wasting daylight and I hope we find this boy before dark. Lord knows last night was cold and rough enough for the guy."

"We gonna stay out here tonight?" Oliver asked.

"You'd like that, wouldn't you?" Alfred Stewart, one of the cowboys who worked for Silas, asked and then grinned.

"We'll spend the night. We've got grub, blankets and gear, so I see no reason to return without the lad." Fred said and then started his horse off at a walk.

*****

George Lee, the man leading the rescuers on the ATV's, had been assigned to check all the trails down to the valley. While it sounded easy enough, there were literally hundreds of miles of trails and only four of them to do the job. They had to move slowly too, in case Mike heard their engines and tried to run to them. His people found it was hard to watch the trail, which wound around the side of the mountain like a twisting snake, look for smoke, and also sign.

Near dark they met at an agreed location to spend the night. As shelters were put up and fires started, Lee said, "I think we need someone riding shotgun to look for sign. I almost rode over the side of this mountain today looking for the boy."

"I had problems too." Bob King, the Emergency Medical Technician, said as he added a small log to the fire.

"Okay, in the morning, before we start our search we'll return to get someone to ride behind us. Try to get someone lightweight and avoid big people. Once we've got spotters, we'll continue our search."

Churchwell Temples asked, "What if this youngster cuts across the woods?" Churchwell was a big man and everyone called him Church. The name Churchwell was too long and he was a deacon, so the name fit. He was also a deeply religious man.

"Church," George said, "why would he do that?"

"I don't know, just askin'."

"Most survivors stay on the easiest route, because like everyone in life, they're lazy. I've been searching for folks for over ten years and only know of one case where the survivor moved overland and left the trails."

"Did he tell you why he'd left the trail?"

"No, it was in the desert, and a horse mounted group found his body. He was a good twenty miles from where we were searching."

"Lawdy, I hope you find this kid alive." Bob King said as he pulled out a dehydrated meal in a pouch.

"This boy is smart and so far the only thing he's done incorrectly is not waiting for us to find him. I suspect he's scared he's in trouble, hungry, tired and more than just a little cold. If he stops long enough, we'll find 'em." Marshall

Creech, another ATV operator, said as he sat on a log beside the dancing flames.

Lee said, "I suggest we all turn in early and get some sleep. It'll be cold tonight, so prepare for it, and I want us up two hours before daylight. Right at daylight, we'll start looking for the young man again."

\*\*\*\*\*

Smith and Silas sat up long after the others had gone to bed and besides, Smith was to guard the horses for two hours, then wake Edwin Hollowman to take over. Unlike ATV's or other motorized vehicles, there were large animals that called these mountains home that would eat a horse. Cougar, bear or even wolves were known to attack horses on a picket line, hoping to dine on a meal of horse flesh.

"You've been a friend of mine for over thirty years, so what's your opinion, honestly, about the odds of us finding this boy alive as cold as it is at night?" Silas asked.

Fred removed his cowboy hat, ran his fingers through his hair and replied, "Dang hard to figure out, really. If the boy stays smart, and I think he will, we'll find him safe and sound. Keep in mind, after a few days, fatigue will climb on his back because he'll have to keep his fire burning to survive the low temperatures at night. That means he'll catnap for an hour, wake up, and feed his constantly hungry fire, then go back to sleep again. He'll get no long sleep while out here, unless it warms up a great deal."

Leaning forward with his forearms on his thighs and a cup of coffee in his hands, Silas replied, "You see it like I do. I give the boy a week."

Giving a dry chuckle, Fred replied, "By golly, this boy might surprise you, and I'm sure he'll last at least two weeks and on guts alone. See, I know this boy's father; Peter and I went to school with Tom, Peter's daddy, and even knew old man Nash when I was a boy. Three generations of the Nash men, and I found not a one less than a real man. Old man Nash got a Silver Star in World War Two and Tom got two Bronze Stars in Vietnam, same unit I was in. Fightin' runs in Nash blood and I mean in every single one of 'em. If it can be done, we'll find this young button alive, but we both know there are times when fightin' and determination ain't enough. I'd surely hate to have to tell Peter we found his boy dead."

"We cain't save 'em all, can we?"

"Nope we can't, but we do find most of 'em alive and while some are hurt, I've seen very few dead. I honestly feel deep down inside, we'll find this child alive."

Silas stood and out of habit, dusted the rear of his jeans off, and then said, "I'm headin' to my bedroll. If you have any problems, let me know."

"I've got my Winchester and you'll hear her speak if I have any problems. G'night, old buddy, and remember Mike Nash in your prayers."

"Oh, I've prayed for the boy and us. I don't care who finds him, but I want all of us looking for him to return home safely. All it'd take is a rock slide, heavy snow storm, or rain, and we could lose some good people. Night, Fred."

After Silas moved to his tent and bedroll, Fred sat by the fire thinking. He'd spent a hitch in search and rescue during the Vietnam War and had the DD-214 as well as the scars to prove it. He'd served four years in the United States Air Force, got out, and then used the G.I. Bill to get his degrees. Most folks were surprised to discover Fred held both a BS in Animal Science and Master's Degree in Bio Resource & Agricultural Engineering. He chuckled as he sat beside the fire, because he dressed in his work clothes all the time and he was a rancher. He wore jeans, boots, gloves and a cowboy hat, but when needed, he could cut a fine figure and look as good as any man, only it really wasn't him. He was the same cowboy he'd been before he'd entered the military, but financially he was stable.

Near the end of his shift, he spotted movement near the horses, but was unable to see what it was. He knew his night vision was messed up, because he'd sat by the fire to stay warm, and now it would take minutes to see if the motion was a threat or not. He placed a live round in the chamber of his 30.30 and waited.

A dark shape ran and was seen as a shadow against the gray sky and Fred lined up the sights and pulled the trigger. The shape was knocked around, and a loud yelp of pain was given. Fred yelled, "Wolves are at the horses!"

Silas and his cowboys, plus one cowgirl, were quickly out of the tents and moving for their mounts. Rifles were heard as they chambered a round. No rancher had ever been attacked by a healthy wolf and unless the animal had rabies, it was unheard of.

Suddenly rifles fired, a horse screamed and a wolf moved to Oliver, where he stood, blood dripping from his teeth as he growled at the young woman.

Scared but holding a rifle, she raised her barrel and fired, knocking the wolf to the ground. The animal attempt to regain his feet, but was unable to do so.

Silas neared and said, "You started it, now finish the job. He'll not survive with his front legs hit like they are."

Saddened, yet knowing her father was right, she sighted the animal in and squeezed the trigger. The shot seemed louder than the others, but the wolf dropped unmoving.

"You did it right, girl, now get over near the horses and check 'em out. I want every animal checked closely for any injury."

"Sure, dad."

"Ben, get a lantern from your tent and look our mounts over closely. Lewis, I want you and Edward to make sure the wolves are all dead and take no chances. If it moves, shoot it. Once you've checked 'em, get some rope and drag 'em off far enough the stink won't bother anyone using the trail."

Fred asked, "Should we call the attack in?"

"Well, let's wait and see how the horses are doing. I'm only to report important things and if the mounts are in good shape, I see no reason to report it to the rescue center. They're busy enough just coordinating all of this."

Ten minutes later as Fred and Silas sat by the fire, Ben called out, "All but one are in excellent shape. Dusty, Lewis' mare, has a hamstring torn and hanging."

Fred met the eyes of Silas as the rancher stood and nodded. Both men knew the animal would never heal normally and they knew of no treatment or cure. Silas chambered a fresh bullet and made his way toward the horses.

A few minutes later, the sound of a shot was heard and then Silas returned with his rifle in his hand. Sitting beside his friend he said, "No matter how many times you have to do the job, it never gets easier." Then, his eyes watered.

"What now?"

"I'll call Rescue Center and let them know we're short a horse. I'll have them send a man to my place tonight, get another horse, and deliver it to us by first light. We'll just have to wait here until the horse arrives."

"What about the body of Dusty?" Fred asked and stoked the flames.

"She'll rest where she fell. We don't have the time or energy to bury her, not when a young man needs our help. If the Rescue Center wants her buried, they'll have to supply the manpower and shovels."

"You're going to bill them for the cost of your animal, aren't you?"

"No, I think not, because I volunteered to be here. If they'd hired me or made me come out here, well, it'd be a different story."

"I hear you." Fred said and then yelled, "Alright y'all, let's get back in the tents. The excitement's over for the night."

# CHAPTER 4

PETE and Wendy were an emotional mess and neither had slept the night before. Peter had sat talking with Barbara Adams and each time the radio would come alive, his hopes lifted, only to be squashed a few seconds later. Finally, the radio operator said, "Mr. Nash, why don't you at least go sit on the sofa and watch TV for a while? I promise, as soon as I hear something about Mike, I'll let you know."

Peter stood and said, "Thanks." *I'm so tired, but I can't sleep until Mike is found,* he thought as he moved toward the TV. *I still can't figure out why he moved once he had a fire and shelter. It makes no sense to me at all.*

Doctor Lemuel Patton was watching the news and he asked, "Do either of you need anything to help you sleep? I hate to say this, but you both look pretty rough."

"I don't want anything." Wendy replied.

"Me either." Peter said.

"Look, you'll not miss anything. Neither of you can continue without sleep for much longer. The pill I have in mind will relax you, but not force you to sleep. I strongly suggest you try it and then sleep if you can. There is absolutely nothing you can do for Mike right now and you're actually harming your bodies. I promise to wake you if anything happens."

Suddenly a photo of Mike was on the news and the reporter said, "Eleven year old Mike Nash is reported missing in the high mountains west of town. Mike, who was with a group of Boy Scouts wandered off while fishing and authorities are currently searching for the missing boy. We have a reporter en-route where we hope to have an exclusive interview with his parents at six o'clock this morning. This is Lee Johnson, with WXXD news."

"I hope you both heard that. Someone is coming to interview both of you, so rest is needed." The doctor said and then smiled.

"Okay, we'll take the drug," Peter said, "but only on the condition news people are kept away from us and if anything, anything at all, is discovered about Mike, you'll wake us."

"Sure, both of your requests sound perfectly normal and reasonable to me. Let me get my bag and I'll be right back."

\*\*\*\*\*

Morning was cold, but dry, and Mike was experiencing severe pain. His whole right arm was swollen to about three times its normal size and each time his heart would beat, he'd feel pain. Delirious most of the night, he wasn't much better this morning, but his hunger was gone. He wasn't worried about food, so he sipped some water from his folding cup, leaned back on his pine boughs and fell asleep; his mind immediately took him far away in a dream . . .

"Mike," Mother asked, "you need to wake up and get dressed. If you remember, we have to be in church a little early, so you can prepare to sing with the choir. Being a new member, you don't want to be late, now do you?"

"W . . . what time is it?"

"Fifteen minutes after six, and the choir is going to practice for a couple of hours before church. Don't you remember any of this?"

Sliding his legs off the bed, he rubbed his eyes and then replied, "I remember, but this is pretty early to be getting up on a Sunday."

"Come on, sleepy head, and eat your breakfast."

At that point, Mike's dream shifted to many different things he remembered as a child. His first camping trip, visiting his grandfather, and school activities, were just a few. While unaware of it, the poison from the snake was taking control of his mind and even his dreams were out of control.

\*\*\*\*\*

George Lee looked into the ravine, shook his head, and then yelled, "Are you okay, Marshall?"

Not a sound was heard.

"We need to get down there and check him out. It's possible he's either seriously hurt or been killed." Bob King said and then added, "Let me get a rope and then I'll go down. If he can't walk or has been killed, we can pull him up using an ATV. I'm sure a helicopter can't even reach him down there, due to all the brush and saplings."

Lee said, "Get the rope, and Churchwell, I need you to back your ATV to the edge of this drop, but not too close or you'll join Creech at the bottom. Dang, of all things, I never expected part of this ledge to give away like it did."

King returned and said, "Relax, George, no one expected it, and it's just one of the hazards of a search. Creech knew the risks, because we all do. Let's just pray he's okay and move on."

"I hear you, Bob, but I'm still responsible for all of you."

"Here, hold this rope while I go down. I should be able to hold onto brush and bushes on the way down, but coming up, even with the ATV helping me might get rough."

George nodded, took the rope and watched as his EMT started down. About half way down the hillside, Bob slipped and would have fallen, if George hadn't been holding the rope.

"You okay?" George yelled.

"I'm fine, and I see Creech moving!"

"Let me know his condition as soon as possible."

Once at the bottom, Bob untied the rope and moved to Creech. The man was laying on his back with his blue eyes open, and then he blinked.

"Are you okay, man?"

"I can't move my legs."

"Any pain there?"

"I don't feel anything from my waist down and the only pain I have is in my head and left arm."

"Well, your helmet has a big gouge in it from hitting something on the way down. Let me move to your arm and check it out." Bob said.

Squatting beside his mate, the EMT saw immediately the arm was broken, because the jagged edge of a bone was pushed through the long shirt sleeve. He was bleeding, but that would be the lesser of his problems to deal with right now.

"How's it look?" Creech asked.

Lying, Bob said, "Not bad, but the arm is broken and I suspect feeling will come back to your legs once a little time passes. Your head may be a different story. I think you have experienced a concussion, but they'll be able to tell once a medivac removes you to a hospital." Then, opening his medical bag, he thought, *Lord, heal his legs and all his injuries. He's too good of a man to spend the rest of his life in a wheelchair.*

"What now?" Creech asked.

"Easy; I'll get George to call the Rescue Center and order a medivac. Once the chopper is here, I'll have them lower a Stokes Litter and then we'll get you out of the bush."

"How's he look?" George called out from the top, worried about his man.

"Get Rescue Center to send a medivac. It looks like a broken arm, concussion and spinal injuries. Tell them I need all the braces to secure the patient; oh, and send a board for his back too."

"Roger, I'll get 'em on the horn."

Churchwell asked, "Do I need to untie the rope?"

"No, leave it in place. One of us may need to go down to help Bob, or he may need to come back up. Let me get a chopper for Creech, because he's in pain." George said and then contacted the Rescue Center. Five minutes later, he yelled, "Bob, the evac is due in twenty minutes!"

"Got ya and it'll be a long twenty minutes for Creech. His adrenaline is wearing off and his pain is growing by the minute."

"Do you have any painkillers?"

"No, nothing heavy like morphine or anything." Bob yelled back.

Suddenly, Creech arched his back and gave a loud soul cutting scream as his body jerked violently. The injured man shrieked, "The pain! I can't take the pain!" Then just as suddenly, his body fell back to the forest floor and all movement stopped.

"I . . . is he . . . he dead?" George asked, his voiced edged with fear.

"No! He has passed out from the pain. I'm treating him for shock right now. When the chopper arrives, I need you and Church to get the Stokes Litter once it touches the ground. Let it touch the dirt first, or the static electricity will knock you on your backside, and I'm not joking. It builds up static as the wench lowers it and it packs a heavy punch. Once you have it, send it down to me using another rope. Once it's here, I'll need one of you to help me move him to the litter."

"Got ya and I'll let you know when the bird nears."

Bob knew from experience that he'd hear the chopper way before he'd see it, but George was likely a bit nervous and he had a valid reason to be. The EMT liked his crew, because each man was an experienced professional in the field. He could count on them.

Fifteen minutes later, George heard his radio come alive, "Wheels One, this is Save One, and I'm nearing your location, over."

"Roger, Save One, I read you five by five. You're as clear as a bell."

"Copy, Wheels. I will attempt to fly over your location, but give me a countdown, so I can mark your exact spot."

"Copy, Save, I'm ready."

The chopper had been flying a 360 path, but now lined up and approached George. Keeping his eyes on the bird and his ears open, just in case trees blocked his view, the man on the ground said, "You're overhead in five, four, three, two, one, now!"

"Copy that now, Wheels, and my spotter has you in view. He saw two or three ATV's on a narrow trail."

"Roger, that's us."

"I can hover above you and lower the Stokes Litter, but allow it to ground out before touching it, copy?"

"Roger that and I copy."

"Do you need a Poppa Juliet?"

George knew a Poppa Juliet was a PJ, or Parachute Jumper, that was trained in survival and emergency medicine. "Negative, we have an EMT in place. I repeat, I have an Echo Mike Tango in place, copy?"

"Copy, Wheels. Good to go then. One slightly used Stokes Litter coming down as soon as we're in position."

"Save One, do you have any painkillers on your aircraft? My EMT has need of them."

"Wait one." the pilot replied and a few seconds later said, "Roger on the painkiller and it'll be tied to the stokes litter, inside the medical bag."

Ten minutes later, the litter was with Bob, and Churchwell stood beside him. Creech was on the litter and a neck brace was attached. The injured man had a shot of morphine and was now out of pain. The chopper had moved off about a half a mile and was seen cutting lazy circles in the air.

"Okay, I have the rope tied to the head of the litter, so pull him up the slope slowly. I will come up at the same time, just in case he gets caught in brush or something. I'll try to keep him moving up. Take it slow, because I think his back is broken."

"Church, I need you up here with me. You'll spot for me as I drive the ATV."

A few minutes later, Churchwell stood near the edge and called out, "Okay, up you come! Yell if you need anything!"

"Will do that!"

George edged the ATV forward as slowly as he could and he heard his spotter saying, "Good, good, little more."

When Creech was about half way up, Churchwell said, "Stop, he's hung up on some brush." Many long minutes passed and then he added, "Okay, move it forward again, slowly."

Less than five minutes later the litter popped up and over the edge. Churchwell helped Bob up and then the two of them raised Creech to flat ground. Bob said, "George, get the medivac to come and fetch their patient."

"Will do, right now."

The chopper returned, lowered the cable, which Bob attached to the litter once it grounded out. Four metal rods ran from the corners of the litter to join at the top in the center right over Creech, and at that location was a ring to be used for attaching a winch hook. Moving away from the litter, Bob gave a thumbs up, and watched as Creech was lifted from the ground. At the door of the helicopter, two airmen pulled the injured man inside the aircraft.

"Wheels One, this is Save One, and your man is inside."

"Roger, Save, and thank you for your assistance." George replied.

"Copy, and keep us in mind if you need us again. This is Save One, out."

Lowering the radio, George said, "Now I need to contact the Rescue Center and let them know Creech is on his way to a hospital. I'm sure they monitored our conversation, but someone will have to let his wife know he's been hurt."

*****

Meanwhile, back at Rescue Center, Wendy was in tears when she'd heard of Creech's injury and felt totally responsible for the mishap. Smith had explained that accidents happen during search and rescues, so she'd better toughen up a little. She was angered by his comment, but said nothing and moved outside to be with friends and family.

"Any change in Creech?" Peter asked as she walked outside.

"He's been picked up by a medical chopper, something called a medivac, and flown to a hospital. His condition is still unknown at this time, other than what the EMT sent by radio to the center."

"Well, there is little we can do now, except pray for the man." May Nash, Peter's youngest aunt said.

Uncle Thomas, a Vietnam War veteran said, "He'll be well cared for in the chopper and in the hospital, unless civilians run the program differently than the military."

"Huh?" Peter said.

"In Tet of 1968 and downtown Saigon, I took a bullet to the back and a medevac chopper took me to a hospital. Once there I was looked over, treated, and then airlifted to Clark Air

Force Base in the Philippines. I think the main reason they sent me to the island was a tough fight was still being fought and some of it right outside the hospital."

"Treated well, huh?" Peter asked.

"No waiting in the emergency room that day for Thomas W. Armstrong, no sir. I was wheeled right in and worked on. I've waited in every emergency room since." Thomas said and then broke out laughing.

Peter laughed, grew serious and then asked, "Who will notify the injured man's family?"

"Trooper Michaels is doing that and he will also take her to the hospital. They've got everything under control, but I wish someone would find my baby."

"I want him found too, but if he hears you called him a baby, he'll get mad. He's a young man and from what little we know, he's doing everything correctly."

Tears flooded her eyes and ran down her cheeks as her body quivered and shook. She tried to smile, but all it did was make her pretty face ugly. She wanted to speak, except she realized talking was out of the question. Her nose started running and she pulled a tissue from her purse.

"Honey," Peter said, "we have to wait, but don't forget whatever happens, is God's will."

"I know that, I really do, but I hope God is feeling merciful with Mike." she was able to get out before she returned to tears once more.

Peter hugged Wendy, pulled her close, and whispered, "I hope so too, baby. I hope so too. No matter what happens, I love you."

\*\*\*\*\*

Darkness found George and his group with a new member, Heather Edwards, as they sat around a small fire. The temperature had gone up and the night was cool, but not cold.

All of them knew Heather; she was assigned to the unit, and this was their first time in the bush with her. She was a quiet woman, who did much more listening and thinking than talking. She wasn't rude, just didn't have much to say most of the time and had little patience for useless chatter.

"Heather, I want you to get to bed early, because we'll be up two hours before sunrise and riding at first light. Now, not to scare you, but there have been reports from our mounted personnel that wolves are active in the area. It seems last night they attacked the horse herd and Silas had to put one down."

"I have a gun." she replied.

"I've seen you on the range and you know how to shoot too. That's all I'm going to say about wolves. Just expect them and if they don't show, it doesn't matter then."

"If they show, you'll hear the shot."

George stood, dusted off his rear, and moved for his tent. He'd lost a man today and it bothered him. He'd lost men before, but Creech was a good friend and they spent a lot of time together. He'd heard nothing from the hospital or Rescue Center and he was apprehensive about his condition. Bob said his back was the most serious injury and it was very possible Creech would never walk again, but he couldn't be sure until some time had passed. Back injuries, like head injuries, were tricky and difficult to diagnose.

George crawled into his sleeping bag and thought, "*God, I rarely ask you for anything, except to bless everyone, including my enemies, but I want you to consider healing Creech. He's a good man, Lord, and you know that, because you know his heart. But, most importantly, God, thy will be done. I'm not a preacher and I've never really been trained on how to talk with you, so I hope you'll take a look into my heart and see I'm in pain. This I ask in the name of Jesus, amen.*" Within minutes, George was asleep.

It was after midnight when Heather moved to the woods to use the 'bathroom,' which was a trench dug into the soft earth, surrounded on four sides with tarps. She knew if she'd not joined the group, the tarps would still be folded and on the ATV's. She'd just started to button her military style pants, when she heard a deep rumbling in the mountain. *There, it did it again,* she thought. *I need to wake George and ask him what that noise is. I still hear it, but it's not as loud now.*

She moved to George's tent and said, "Mr. Lee, I'm hearing a strange noise from the mountain."

A minute later, George stepped from his tent, rubbed his sleepy eyes, and as he ran his fingers through his hair, his eyes grew huge. Turning, he screamed, "Everyone up and on your ATV, now! Hurry! Follow me when you leave! Hurry, not much time!"

The men stumbled from their small tents and Bob asked, "What's going on?"

"I'm not sure and I might be crazy, but I just felt the earth moving and heard noises on the mountain, now mount your ATV!"

"What about all our gear?" Churchwell asked as his ATV started.

"Leave it and follow me, *now!*" George zoomed down the trail at a breakneck speed and knew what he was doing was dangerous, only they had to get out into the open. Unknowingly, he drove right by the sleeping form of Mike, less than twenty feet off the trail.

The last in the group, Heather heard a deep rumble and saw huge boulders rolling toward her. She gave her ATV full throttle, but it coughed and then died. She didn't have time to attempt a restart, so she jumped from the seat, and ran down the trail.

Rocks were bouncing off trees, boulders were knocking trees over like bowling pins and it was

then she felt a blow to her head and she went out like a light, only to fall to the trail —unconscious.

Seeing a large field, on the mountain side, George drove to the middle and counted the ATV's behind him. *Dang! Missing Heather!* he thought and then asked, "Did anyone see where Heather went?"

"She was right behind me." Bob said, "or was the last time I looked."

"When was that?"

"We started moving late and rocks were already coming down the hill and bouncing around, so I took off, but I think she was with me to the first curve. George, to be honest, I have no idea once I started moving how far she followed me, because I didn't look back. I was scared to death."

"Okay, I understand, because it unnerved all of us. I pray she wasn't still in camp when the rocks hit, or she's dead."

"Oh, sweet Jesus, no. Oh, please, God, save her." Churchwell begged as he looked to the heavens.

"Church, his will has already been done and while I can understand your fear right now, Heather is either dead or alive, depending on what the good Lord had planned for her life. At first light, we'll head back and look for her."

Bob said, "I'll get a fire started."

It was then, George gave a light chuckle and said, "Good, because we don't have a radio to talk with Rescue Center."

"W . . . what?" Churchwell asked.

"When I felt the quake and the rumbling of the mountain, I knew we had to move, and quickly. I left it behind."

"So, what now?" Bob asked.

"We look for Heather in the morning and then return to the trailer for a new radio."

# CHAPTER 5

THINGS were hopping in the Rescue Center, with reports of an earthquake and rock slides from all areas around the mountain. Some men and women were missing, others were injured, and there was at least one volunteer killed. The radio operator was now busy and the center was sending out rescue teams to rescue the original rescuers. John Smith was about to pull his hair out, but Barbara was business as usual when using the radio, except the number of communications had jumped through the roof.

John said, "Barbara, tell everyone, on all channels, that only life and death situations need to be called in until further notice. I have a chopper coming in to assist us, but a cold front is moving in and will be here by midnight. If it snows or rains pretty heavy, the aircraft will be grounded."

"I'll let 'em know, sir."

"Any word on the ATV team? Uh, Wheels One is the team I'm looking for, right?"

"Yep, that's the team. Nope, not a sound from them, and a search team on foot reported their night position was covered with boulders, rocks and sand. It doesn't look good."

"Oh, Lord, we don't need more deaths."

"John, I have a whole slew of reporters out here and they're wanting to speak with someone about the Nash boy and this earthquake situation." Frank, one of the supply men, said as he stuck his head in the door.

"Where is the spokesperson from the CAP?"

"He's out in the field. The only reason you have any men left is we're all over sixty and not as spry as we used to be. Some of us older men stayed behind to get supplies and gear ready. We lost a lot of stuff on this mountain."

"Tell the reporters I'll be out in ten minutes to give a briefing. Let them know I will answer no questions at the end."

"Got it, and I'll let them know." Frank replied and then shut the door.

"Oh, I dread this."

"John, just go out and tell them the truth." Barbara replied.

"News folks twist the truth to meet their professional agendas. I'd rather face a room of tigers than a single news reporter."

Barbara smiled, but didn't reply.

"John?" Frank stuck his head in the door.

"What now, Frank?"

"They want to speak with the Nash folks too."

"Alright, I'll take care of it, and Frank?"

"Yep?"

"Thanks."

Frank shut the door and then chuckled. He knew how John felt about news teams and he felt the same way. They'd twist something out of context and use it to meet their purpose.

Ten minutes later to the second, the trailer door opened and John stepped out. Giving an ill-felt smile, he walked to the podium and microphones.

He cleared his throat, took a sip of water and said, "Last night, at approximately midnight, our area was struck by an earthquake. We are currently investigating our losses in lives and gear. We have no idea of the extent of damage done and I can make no other comments at this time."

A female reporter asked, "So, are you saying you did experience fatalities then?"

"I cannot confirm or deny we had any fatalities as this time. I can make no other comments on our status, other than to say I'm not so much concerned about the dead as I am our injured and missing. They will be given our priority when found."

"What of the Nash boy?" another voice asked.

"What about him?" John asked, glad to be away from discussing the quake.

"Will the rescue continue now or be dropped due to the quake?"

"When we started this search, we had every reason to suspect the young man was still alive. We will continue our search."

"For the boy's body, you mean?"

"We have no idea if the quake affected the young man or not, but it's business as usual for us."

"You just stated, 'we had every reason to suspect the young man was still alive.' The key word here is 'had', so does this mean you no longer think he's alive?"

"Let me be blunt, because I think that's the best way to answer your question. We will search for Mike and we will bring him or his body off this mountain."

"Can we speak with the boy's parents, uh, the Nash family? I mean, you're not willing to discuss the quake and the deaths your unit experienced."

John shook his head in frustration and then met Peter's eyes, and he nodded.

"Mr and Mrs Peter Nash, the parents of Mike Nash." John said and then stepped back.

Once standing in front of the press, a portly reporter in front asked, "Ma'am, how did you feel when first notified of Mike being lost?"

"Like any mother, I was and still am deeply concerned and scared for my son."

The reporter nodded and then asked, "Why has it taken so long to find your boy? Is there a problem we're not aware of, or has the situation changed?"

Peter growing irritated already asked, "Do you spend any time in the woods, sir?"

"Well, no, I'm not the outdoors type."

"I can clearly see that. Uh, the woods are not like your home or office, sir, with brush, trees, rocks and steep mountain slopes that must be checked. Often, a person is difficult to find, and it takes time. If the survivor is injured, the search becomes even more difficult."

"So, you have evidence to suggest Mike has been injured, then?"

"No, I have no evidence to suggest he's been injured or not. We were told that an earlier camp he'd used overnight was found and it showed he'd displayed good survival skills at that time. Other than that, I have nothing else to add."

"What will you do now, I mean, well, until Mike is found?"

"We'll stay right here until our son is found. What would you do, sir, if your son was missing?"

"I'm not married, but I imagine I'd wait for him to be found."

Peter nodded as he thought, some of these questions are so stupid. *How do they think we felt when Mike went missing? What do they think we'll do now?*

"Is there anything you'd like say to our readers, sir?"

"Yes, I'd like to asked all of your readers to pray for the safe return of our son."

John noticed the reporters looking at each other and only a few took note of his comment. As the leader, John Smith, moved to the side of the Nash family and said, "That concludes our statements for today and we'll have another briefing tomorrow at the same time. As new information on the quake or the missing child comes available, we'll release it immediately. Thank you." He gave a casual wave of his hand.

When John entered the trailer just a few minutes later, Barbara said, "Still no sign of Wheels One and some of the others. So far, thank God, only one confirmed dead and three missing. I suspect, those people missing may never be found, unless they bring cranes in and check under some big rocks."

"We'll worry about the missing, but only after we recover those alive and confirmed dead. We can help the living and recover the dead."

"John, you need to see this!" Frank yelled from the living room of the trailer.

John moved to the TV and stood as a reporter said, "John Smith, the director and coordinator for the Search and Rescue Center who are currently looking for the missing Nash boy, said today that he's not worried about any dead he has as a result of the quake last night. I was rather stunned by his comment, and he then refused to answer any questions pertaining to his losses or condition of his searchers. His answer to any or all questions about his teams were, quote, 'I can make no other comments at this time,' unquote. While I'm not sure, it appears to be some sort of cover-up involving the rescue efforts being made and the physical state of those who are looking for the missing Nash child. We'll provide additional updates as they become available. This is Gene Hutto, Channel 52 News, reporting. Back to you, Shirley."

"What!" John exploded.

"Boss, chill and let it go. You and I both knew when you walked out the door they'd twist your words. I was there and heard every word spoken." Frank said.

*****

Lee waited until full daylight and then said, "Okay, we'll head back to look for Heather and see if we can salvage any gear we left behind."

Within a few minutes they were moving slowly up a narrow winding trail, which was peppered with rocks of various sizes. Many times they had to ride around, or physically remove, some larger rocks or logs blocking their way. Trees had been knocked over by large boulders, while the big stones had continued to roll down the mountainside, leaving a trail of broken timber.

They drove as near to their old campsite as possible and then turned off their machines and dismounted. All of them feared for the life of Heather, because the mountain side was covered with rocks.

Movement was seen in the rocks and for a moment hope fluttered in their hearts, but a cowboy suddenly appeared standing on a boulder the size of a house.

"Lee, it's me, Silas!'

"Silas, what are you doing on this side of the mountain?" Lee asked.

"Lookin' for you. The Rescue Center contacted us by radio and said they've been unable to reach you. They asked us to try and find you."

"My radio, most of our gear, and Heather Edwards are missing."

Silas and some of his men moved closer to Lee. Finally, the rancher said, "Pard, we've been here since an hour before sun up and haven't seen hide nor hair of another soul, until y'all showed. If Heather is under these rocks, and she very well could be, she's a goner."

"Can I borrow your radio to call Center?"

Tossing the brick sized radio, Silas replied, "Sure."

As Lee spoke to center, the rancher said, "I need everyone, include you folks with ATV's, to start searching for any sign of the missing woman. Give a yell if you find anything."

Lee had just lowered the radio, his reporting in complete, when Bob yelled, "I've some blood over here!"

Fred yelled, "Keep everyone away from the area until Silas and I have a chance to see any sign."

The two old hunters and ranchers had the most experience of anyone in the group and it took Fred just a few minutes of looking before he said, "This looks bad. The blood trail leads to this huge boulder and if she's under here, well, there's no hope at all."

"You sure?" Churchwell asked.

"Son, I was hunting bear and cougar in these mountains before your daddy was born and while I ain't a learned man, I can read sign well enough. The trail leads west and that whole area is nothing but rocks. Unless Heather veered off at the last second or grew wings, she's dead."

"Oh, Lord, and her parents are such good folks, too." Benjamin said.

"Son, I don't mean to sound cold, because I really ain't, but life is hard out here. In all my sixty-two years of life, if I've learned nothin' else, I learned that bad things can happen to good folks too. How-some-ever, if y'all are prayin' folks, now would be a good time to talk to Jesus and pray she moved away from this rock slide at the last minute. I have to be honest, I don't see any sign of her, except leadin' to the rocks."

"Do you know of any other fatalities?" Lee asked.

"Well, Henry Holmes was found dead, with his whole body covered with a boulder, except his head. If it makes a difference, the doctor said he'd taken a blow to the head before he died, so he never knew what hit him." Silas said.

"Henry is dead?" Edward asked and then blinked rapidly a few times.

"You were a friend of his, right, Ed?" Oliver asked, her tone reflecting her concern.

Edward moved to a rock and sat before he replied, "Yes, ma'am, I went to school with 'em, we joined the army together, and we both married a week apart. I can't believe he's dead. Are they sure?"

"I'm not saying this to be ugly, but no one can survive a rock the size of a house on them. He's gone, Ed." Silas said and then placed a hand on his cook's shoulder. Edward Hollowman was a good man and a loving Christian fellow too. Silas hadn't meant to mention Henry's death at all, except it'd slipped out while talking with Lee. Officially, the death was still unconfirmed, since they had to do an autopsy to legally declare the man deceased. *What a mess,* Silas thought, *when a good man has a big rock on him and they hesitate to declare him dead. Henry, you'll be missed, ole son, and by more than just Edward.*

Lee said, "Silas, contact Rescue Center and let them know Heather Edwards is missing and presumed dead. Let them know her trail led to a boulder, where it abruptly stopped. We'll continue searching for her remains, but the rock slide may prevent the removal or finding of her body."

"I'll do that, but what will you do now? Will you keep looking for Mike or return for supplies?"

Giving a dry chuckle, Lee said, "We have to return to camp, because we don't have as much as a blanket among us. I mean no food, no guns, backpacks, or even a radio."

"Not a problem, and I'll let them know."

"Okay, guys let's get moving back to the trailer. The sooner we return, the sooner we can get back here."

"Lee, the Nash search is still active, but we're to place a priority on finding searchers, if possible."

"Any others missing on this side of the mountain that you know of?"

"One man, uh," and pulling a piece of paper from his shirt pocket he said, "David Wood, who was with one of the groups on foot. They were down lower, near Baldy Lake. There may be others missing, but that's the only name I got when I called in early this morning."

"Come on, guys, let's return to the main camp. Thanks for the name of the missing man, Silas."

\*\*\*\*\*

At the Rescue Center, as Frank pulled supplies for the ATV riders, John said, "It'll take days to get the boulder off of Henry and we have a total of four missing, or so it seems. Besides your Heather, we have Linda Link, D.W. Rogers and David Wood, all missing. Now, they may turn up in a day or two, but for right now, look for any blood sign or anything that might indicate someone moved through the area."

Lee thought for a moment and then asked, "Is that weather front still expected to hit tonight?"

John's lips grew tight and his eyes narrowed. Finally, after about a minute, he gave a sigh and replied, "Yep, no change in the weather, so that may cause problems for any survivors."

"I know when we left our camp we either had it on us, or it was crushed. That may mean some of the missing will be facing hard times, if they're still alive. Can they determine if it's snow or rain we'll get?"

"From the earlier news, we'll get freezing rain mixed with snow, followed by either hard rains or heavy snow. That means if the temperatures are at or below freezing we'll get snow, and we'll get rain if it's warmer. I don't think they really know what to expect right now, except winds are expected to be over fifty miles an hour. If we get winds that high, all searching will grind to a halt."

"Frank, make sure we've got a lot of coffee. If the weather turns nasty, not much we can do but wait it out, and I refuse to do that with no coffee."

Frank laughed and once sober, he said, "I'll do without a lot of things in life, but a hot drink on a cold day ain't one of 'em. I'll add an extra pound or so. As a surprise, I'm packing up a half dozen books for y'all too. If it turns rough, you can sip coffee and read a book."

"Good, because passing time whittlin' on pine gets old after a few hours."

Barbara stuck her head out the door and said, "John, they just found the body of D. W. Wood and Linda Link was discovered sitting in the middle of the trail with a possible concussion. They've recovered Mr. Wood and Linda is being brought here from the mountain by horse. Cowboy One said his medical man has treated her and they're moving toward base."

"Did he give an estimated time of arrival?"

"No, but I don't think he can yet. Many of the trails are covered with rocks and trees."

"Okay, contact him and ask if Linda needs immediate medical care. We'll decide on what action to take once he lets us know. I'm inclined to have him wait and send a medivac to him. I consider any head injury as severe."

"Sure, but give me a couple of minutes to get him on the horn again."

Lee said, "Why don't you go in there and take care of business, John? Heather will either turn up, be spotted, or she won't. I hope I'm wrong, but I feel pretty strongly she's under the rock slide."

"We'll know more in a day or two. Yep, I need to get back in, because things are busy today. I'm just glad we didn't lose more people than we did."

"God had a hand in the whole mess."

"It sure looks like it. Give us a radio call once you're back in place. We'll check your radio and pass on any weather info at that time. Take care and stay safe, Lee."

"I will, John, and the same to you. Come on boys, it's time to head back into the mountains."

\*\*\*\*\*

An hour later, as they moved along the winding snake-like trail that meandered on the side of the mountain, Bob said, "It's snowing."

Lee looked up and spotted a few flakes and knew then they'd get little rain. *Lord, let any of our missing get to a fire and shelter, please. Cover them and protect them with your hands, God.*

# Chapter 6

HEATHER was in serious pain and she had no idea where she was. Her vision was cloudy, her head was pounding, and she was stumbling down a beaten path, but in what direction she had no idea. She didn't even know who she was, why she was in the woods, or how she got there. Blood flowed freely from her head and while she knew she needed to bandage the wound, her arms didn't seem to want to obey her commands and her feet wanted to keep moving. *Why the strong urge to move,* she thought, *Am I in danger and don't realize it?*

She'd awakened in a cloud of dust and flying debris, totally confused, and the urge to move quickly had been with her since. It was then she smelled wood smoke.

There is a fire near and maybe someone to help me. *It's starting to snow and it's grown colder,* she thought as she sniffed the wind. *That way.*

She neared a rough looking camp, the shelter made of pine limbs, a small fire, and a young boy sleeping near the flickering flames. She saw no gear, no food and no water, but a fire was enough for her at the moment. The boy made an alarm in her mind ring, only she had no idea why. *Oh, my, his arm is injured,* she thought as she saw the swollen limb. *I need to care for me, then look him over.*

Out of her group of searchers, she was the only one that carried a small fanny packet on her belt. She removed it, pulled out a first aid kit, and removed a roll of gauze. She then removed a small towelette of alcohol and cleaned her injury with clinched teeth. *Oh, that hurts,* she thought and never realized her years of study and involvement in CAP, as well as search and rescue, was all that was keeping her alive. She was functioning without really thinking. She did notice her urge to run was gone, only she didn't understand why.

Once her head was wrapped, she moved to the boy and looked him over. When she spotted the fang marks she thought, *He wasn't bitten today, too cold, so it had to be yesterday when it happened. Not much I can do for a snakebite, except give him an over the counter painkiller and keep feeding him water. Who is this boy? He means something to me, but I don't think he's family.*

The painkiller helped her a little, but she still hurt as she gathered wood and then returned to camp. She'd collected enough wood for a day or two, but right now she needed to see what they had on hand to help them to survive.

Sitting by the fire, she found her telephone in her pocket, so opening it, she saw the light come on. She didn't remember a single name or number, so she started reading the face of her phone. She opened the saved numbers and saw a long line of names, but not a one meant anything. It was then she saw Dr. Katherine Jones, and felt good with the name. Is this my doctor? I need to call the number and see if I can get us out of here. She pushed the call button and waited.

Suddenly a voice on the phone said, "Doctor Jones' office. Press one for appointments, press two for the nurse, press three to speak with the lab. If you're a representative for a pharmaceutical firm, we do not accept unsolicited inquiries over the phone. Please make your selection now or push pound five to repeat the choice options."

"Hello! We're hurt in the woods and need help!" While the phone remained silent, Heather grew angry. *I need to choose a number!* she suddenly realized. She then pushed number five to hear her selection choices once again. She suddenly pushed number one and waited.

"Welcome to the office of Doctor Jones, we're experiencing a larger than normal number of calls, so please hold. If you'd rather hold without music, push pound five now."

"Answer, now!" Heather screamed as she waited.

About five minutes later, a woman answered, "Hello, my name is Sally and how may I help you today?"

"Sally, I need help. I'm in the woods and have a head injury. There is a young boy with me and he's been bitten by a snake. His arm is all swollen and he looks bad."

"Who are you? If you have an emergency, please hang up and dial 911."

"Sally you know me, I'm, uh, well, I don't remember my name, but I think Doctor Jones is my doctor."

"Is this a gag of some sort? Listen, I'm very busy right now, so call someone else to get a laugh out of, okay?"

"No, please, don't hang up!"

Sally hung up and began pushing papers. Doctor Jones walked in with coffee in her hand and asked, "Why so rude?"

"Some idiot just called playing games with me."

"Oh, and what was said? I hope they kept it clean."

"It was a woman and she said she had a head injury, didn't know who she was, and she was in the woods with a boy. She said she thought she was one of your patients. Now get this, the boy had been bitten by a snake, too."

"It's possible if she does have a head injury she might not remember her name or any other details about herself. Listen, I think this was a gag too, but run a quick computer check of her phone number and see if it's linked to a patient of mine. It's the last call received."

Sipping her scalding coffee, Doctor Jones waited until Sally said, "I'll be darned. The number belongs to a Heather Edwards; do you remember her?"

"Yep and she'd been a patient of mine for over seven years. This was no gag, because she gets an annual physical for the Search and Rescue organization she's helping as a volunteer. I need you to call the police, while I try to call her back."

The doctor called and Heather answered almost immediately, "Hello."

"Heather, this is Doctor Jones. Are you in some kind of trouble or need help?"

"My head hurts and I'm with a boy that was bitten by a snake. I don't know who I am or where I'm at, except I'm surrounded by trees." At that point, Heather broke down and began crying.

"Heather! Heather, listen to me. Heather, I want to help you, but you must help me too." The doctor then covered the phone, turned to Sally and said, "Tell the police I have her on the line and it's a valid emergency."

"W . . . what do . . . you want me to do?"

"Heather, have you treated your head injury and checked the boy?"

"I cleaned my head with alcohol and his fang marks, too. I'm scared about him because I think he's dying. I wrapped my head and his arm. He's badly swollen." Heather was not aware her speech was slurred and slow at times, but the doctor was concerned.

"Heather, can you stay on the line with me as the police try to determine your location?"

"I'll —"

"Heather? Heather, can you hear me?" the doctor asked and then looking at Sally she said, "I think she passed out. Are the police working this?"

"They're still on the line."

"I'll call her back and see if she'll respond. I hope so." She pushed the numbers but got a quick message that said service was not available for that area. Doctor Jones grew angry, because she'd just spoken with Heather. She sat down, unknowingly sipped her coffee, and said, "This is not good. She's not sounding well and now I've lost contact with her."

\*\*\*\*\*

"John, the police are on the phone and it's about Heather! I think you need to take this call and now. They claim someone has spoken to her."

"This is John." he said when he picked up the phone.

A few minutes later, he stood and said, "Heather's doctor got a call from her, so we know she's alive. She lost contact, either from her injury or connection and wasn't very helpful to the doctor. The doctor, uh —" he then picked up a tablet of paper, "Jones, said she'd experienced a head injury and didn't remember anything. But, the important thing is, I think she found Mike Nash."

"Good, let's go get them." Frank said and then gave a goofy grin.

"Well, that's the problem. See, the police looked up her telephone records and found where the call was made, but they don't know the exact location. All they could tell me was it was near Baldy Lake, on our mountain. With the bad weather already here, we can't do a thing and even if the weather was good, it wouldn't be an easy or fast rescue."

Barbara said, "I don't understand. If she called 911, they'd know exactly where she is right now."

"She called her doctor and according to Doctor Jones, Heather's speech was slow and slurred, almost as if she were drunk. According to the good doctor, it's typical for someone who's had a bad head injury."

"Is she in danger of dying on us?" Frank asked.

"Well, I'll be honest with both of you. Jones told the police that depending on the extend of her injury, she might be hemorrhaging right now, or have swelling of the brain. If either happens, yes, she could die."

"Where does Mike fit into all of this?" Barbara asked.

"I have no idea, but Heather stated she was with a young boy that was bitten by a snake. Doctor Jones said from Heather's comments, it was a poisonous snake. The boy's bitten arm is puffed up pretty good. Before she could learn more, well, they lost the connection or our rescuer passed out."

"How far could a person with a head injury travel?" Frank asked.

"Now, that's an excellent question, for which I have no answer. Keep in mind, she'd be likely moving downhill and that alone would make movement easier. So, honestly, your guess is as good as mine. Now, the doctor said she thinks she heard a fire burning and popping in the background as Heather spoke. She's not sure, but we do know she's alive, or was as recently as two hours ago."

Frank looked out the window, saw snow falling sideways from the high winds, and said, "Oh, look at the storm, and ain't neither of them dressed for this kind of weather."

John ignored Frank and said, "Barbara, look up Heather's number; it's on her personnel sheet, and every thirty minutes give her a call. I want you to keep doing this until you either make contact with her or I tell you to stop. Around the clock, okay?"

"Sure, John, and I'll write it in my log book so when Katie relieves me, she'll do the same."

John looked out the window and said, "Frank, see if Reverend Brooks is in his trailer. I think we may need some divine intervention right now. When all else fails, call on the lord, that's what my momma always says."

"She's right, you know." Barbara said.

"Of course, she's a mother, and a woman."

Barbara broke out laughing as Frank opened the door and entered the storm in search of their man of God.

\*\*\*\*\*

Silas and his men were worried about the horses and finally fought the high winds to make a tarp windbreak to keep the animals warmer.

Moving to the fire, Edward said, "I've been in the woods most of my life and I've never seen it as cold as it is now."

"It's cold enough for the sap in trees to freeze, so if you hear a loud pop tonight, almost like a gunshot, that's what is making the noise. But, on the positive side, the rocks don't have coats on yet, so there is still hope." Silas said.

Everyone laughed and then Benjamin said, "I was stationed in Alaska for three years, with the Army, and it gets bitter cold there. The coldest I saw there was minus seventy. When the weather hit the freezing mark, it actually felt warm, so you'd see Alaskans walking around in tee-shirts and shorts. Nonetheless, it was freezing."

"I hear it's a beautiful place, but I'd not like the weather." Silas replied as he poured coffee into

his beat-up tin cup. "This is way too cold for me, but we have people to look for, so I'll put up with it for a few days." He then took a sip of his hot drink.

Oliver asked, "What do you think about the phone call Heather made?"

Silas chuckled and when sober said, "I'm not laughing at her injury, not at all, but she stumbles on the boy while the rest of us are looking for him like a pack of bloodhounds. The odds of that are remote. Her head injury has me worried, because they're serious business, and the Nash boy has been snake bit."

"Yep," Benjamin agreed, "so neither is fully able to help the other. Not good at all. I do think Heather's training will come out though, hurt or not."

"I sure hope so, because tonight it'll be needed and then some. This is one rough storm for this time of the year, and the first snow since spring thaw."

"The wind chill makes it well below zero right now."

"Relax, we've got insulated sleeping bags, as well as some of the best gear on the market. We'll survive, but what about those two?   From what I understand the boy was wearing hiking shorts." Alfred Stewart said what was really on everyone's mind.

"I'm tellin' all of you right now, if anyone could survive this, it will be Heather. She's pretty and petite, but hard as nails, guys.  Don't let the fact she's a woman or small influence your thinking.  Remember, Napoleon was small too."  Benjamin said and then added, "I've trained with her and she's sharp."

Standing, Silas said, "I'm calling it a night. We will pull two hour shifts of guard on the horses tonight, just as we've been doin' since the wolves attacked. I want all of you well rested in the morning, because if this wind dies, we search." He then moved to his tent and sleeping bag.

\*\*\*\*\*

Lee stood shaking in the trees as he relieved himself and moaned as the pressure in his bladder grew less. He watched the steam from his urine and thought, *I don't see how Mike will survive this cold snap, with or without Heather. If I remember correctly, she was wearing a windbreaker, jeans, boots and a ball cap when I saw her last. I do know what she had on is all she has now. I'm glad she's alive, but for how long? If her head injury doesn't kill her, it's likely this cold will. Very unusual weather for this time of the year. I need to get back to camp and get everyone ready for sleep.*

He walked to camp, squatted by the dancing flames and then held his palms toward the heat.

"Spit it out, Lee.  I've been working rescue with you for over ten years and you're working something in your mind."  Fred said, as he looked over the rim of his tin cup.

"I'm worried, Fred, and have good reason to do the job. It's a record setting low temperature right now, for this time of the year, and we have two survivors who are ill prepared for this kind of weather."

Sitting his almost empty coffee cup by his foot, Fred replied, "Ain't a thing we can do to help them, or we'd already be doing it. You seem to forget that Heather is one of us and as such, she's been well trained. Now, Mike, he's a Boy Scout with Merit Badges galore, so relax a little."

"Yep," Churchwell said, "They'll not be comfortable, but if they get out of the wind and have a couple of fires, they'll be warm enough. I don't think they'll do much sleeping this night, 'cause they'll be feeding the fire to keep warm."

Bob started to say something, but must have changed his mind. When he saw Lee looking at him, he said, "Church, you're not considering that both of them have serious injuries. We have no idea of the extent of Heather's head injury and I've seen some bad ones as an EMT. She might need years of recovery and therapy, just to be able to speak clearly. As for Mike and his bite, it won't likely kill him, but there are a lot of variables that come into play with snakes. Both injuries, depending on their severity, can potentially kill."

"Well, with his arm swelling we know it was a poisonous snake, no doubt. Now, with all my years in this area, I'd say a timber rattler, but that's just a guess." Fred said and then continued, "He's lucky the snake bit a limb, because if it had got him in the face or neck, he'd likely be dead right now."

"Most snakebites occur to arms, legs, hands, and feet, I think I read something like 95%, but I might be wrong. He's healthy, according to Rescue Center, and Doctor Patton gave the boy an excellent chance of surviving the bite. Now, survival is one thing, surviving with deep pain is another. If Heather has any painkillers on her, we all know they'll be over the counter stuff and not strong enough to reduce Mike's pain by much." Bob met the eyes of each person around the fire as he spoke.

"What happens when a person has bad pain and can't find any relief? I don't have much medical training, except some survival medicine and gunshot wounds training." Churchwell said.

"Well, a lot depends on the person." Bob said and then added, "Because we're all different and take pain differently. With that said, it's important to remember, we all have a limit to how much suffering we can take. Some will pass out numerous times over the course of a day, others will be unconscious most of the time, while still others will experience delirium and be useless."

"What about a serious head injury?" Churchwell asked.

"It can kill. We have no idea if Heather's brain has been injured and by that I mean if her brain was punctured or ripped, or even if it's bleeding or swelling. I suspect she's the more serious of the two, because according to what Lee told me, her speech was badly slurred and her memory was gone." Bob said and then stood. He dusted his butt off and said, "I'm heading to bed. We can sit here all night and discuss our survivors, but it'll do no good until we find them. G'night." He then walked from the fire toward his tent.

The remaining men by the fire were quiet for a long time and then finally Churchwell asked, "You don't reckon she'll spend the rest of her life drooling down her chin and making baby noises, do you?"

He was answered with silence.

# CHAPTER 7

HEATHER was shaking violently and had never been as cold as she was right now. She'd moved Mike closer to the fire and covered him with her windbreaker. She was adding more wood to increase the size of the flames. As the flames grew, she wondered why her phone no longer worked. She'd lost the signal when talking to someone, but couldn't remember who. She'd placed the phone beside her, still on, and spent the day feeding always hungry flames. Now the light on her phone didn't come on and she had no idea why it didn't work. She was having trouble thinking; both her short and long term memory didn't work well, and words wouldn't form well in her mind.

Mike had awakened at some point during the day, only he'd made little sense, thinking Heather was his mother. He'd told her he was scared of dying, was in pain, and thirsty. She'd given him water to drink and then he'd gone back to sleep. She had no idea how she'd ended up with a boy, and couldn't remember if she was married with children or not.

Suddenly, she felt a sharp pain in her head, right over her left eye. She grabbed her head, gave a light scream, and then fell to the dirt beside the flickering flames.

Heather had no idea how long she was unconscious, but when she came around the fire was low, almost out, and the winds high. She added logs to the flames and then stared off into space. Something took over and she pulled the skinning knife she carried on her belt and began to cut boughs from pines. Soon, she'd circled the whole camp with a wall pine boughs and while some wind got through the limbs, much of it was blocked. Freezing, she returned to the fire and sat in the dirt. Snow was still falling, but the accumulation didn't amount to much yet.

She glanced up at the sky, which brought pain, but all she could see was low dark gray clouds and falling snow. She leaned over, checked Mike and saw he was breathing and unlike yesterday, it was deep and even. Last night the young man was breathing hard and irregular, which scared her, even though she was unsure why she feared his breathing rate. Something in her mind was warning her to watch his breathing and to keep him warm.

She pulled his pack to her, removed all his gear and pulled out his hiking shorts. Pulling her knife, she cut the shorts right up one side and then covered his legs with the canvas material. Once the material was on him, it was fairly long and flat, but not very wide. It would have to do, because that's all she had.

She pulled part of the windbreaker from Mike's arm and to her, it appeared some of the swelling had gone down. She was not aware she was smiling when she covered the boy again, but she was sure Mike was getting better; she felt it inside. She looked his food over and placed half of a peanut butter sandwich on the ground beside her, as well as the chocolate bar and three hard candies. She had no food, so that was all they had until found.

Long cold hours passed and at midday it was still snowing, so she woke Mike and fed him half of the peanut butter sandwich, then saved the remainder for him to eat later. He didn't want to eat or drink, but she forced him. She opened the chocolate bar and ate two small squares, allowing them to melt in her mouth. The chocolate squares were so rich and tasty that she was tempted to eat more, but resisted and placed it back in the pack with the sandwich.

She took Mikes metal cup, scooped up some snow and placed the metal container near the fire, hoping to melt the snow. She forgot about it seconds later, while she tried her phone again. After a bit, with the phone no longer working, she saw the snow in the cup had melted, so she took a sip. It was hot and by the time she finished the drink, she felt warmer inside. She then packed the cup with snow and placed it beside the fire to melt, so she could feed some to Mike.

She'd just added a small log to her fire, when she heard a noise. Heather was usually armed when in the bush, but during the rock slide she'd lost her pistol, so all she had was an empty holster. The noise sounded again, which filled her with apprehension. She listened to the movement, but all she knew was it was big and moving nearer to their camp. She picked up a log and prepared herself for a fight. She had no idea what animals were in the woods, but this was no squirrel. She was unable to fight big animals anyway, and all she knew was something big was nearing.

She stood, which gave her a dizzy spell, and held her rough club in both hands. The noise was closer now.

Her stomach felt like it had a small animal inside, chewing. *There, I heard it again,* she thought as she glanced out into the falling snow toward the noise. She squinted her eyes, hoping to see better and fear was about to get the best of her. It was then a doe and her yearling stepped into plain view. Heather gave a loud sigh of relief and dropped the club from her hands. She was unable to think of the word deer, but knew the animal would not hurt her. As soon as her club struck the ground, the deer took off and in two or three bounces, they were gone.

She sat back on the ground and began to cry uncontrollably and prayer never entered her mind, because she was unable to remember Him or even her church. Rocking from side to side, with her arms crossed, tears rolled from her eyes. Her emotional breakdown brought on a severe headache and she was soon asleep beside the fire.

\*\*\*\*\*

John sat in his corner of the trailer, or as he called it, his office, and gave the CAP spokesman a strange look and then asked, "How do we explain that Heather is with Mike without giving out too much information?"

"John, they need to know that Mike is with an adult now." Dave Morgan replied. Dave was a portly man with thinning hair and bad teeth. He'd retired from a local TV station two years ago and now worked with the CAP.

"Agreed, but do they need to know she's likely of little help?"

"Listen to me. The truth has to come out and it will eventually. I can buy you 48 hours by stalling a bit, but not an hour more, okay?"

"Look, I'm not asking you to lie to the reporters, just don't say all we know yet. We've been unable to reach Heather's parents, and they don't need to hear this on the news first; we have no idea of her current medical condition, and we don't even know if she and Mike are surviving this storm."

"Okay, I'll go along with this for today and tomorrow, but I think it'd be a good idea to keep the Nash folks in here when I speak to the press. If one of them should accidentally bring up Heather, things will pop us all in the rear and fast, too. They'll immediately accuse us of a cover-up and that's really not the case."

"Okay, just let them know that a rescuer is with the boy, but due to the storm, we're unable to continue our operations."

"John, while that's not a lie, it's hardly the truth. With Heather in the condition she's in, she may be a hardship on Mike. No, I'll leave all of the new information out of the nightly report. I'll simply state that we have no new announcements and most likely won't have until the front passes. That is the absolute truth, because we're simply not announcing what we cannot confirm."

Peter neared as Dave was leaving and asked, "Any idea when this storm will pass?"

"Our weather team says in a day or two. It all depends on when it's shoved along by another front that is behind this one."

"Snow or rain in the next front?"

"It's been only rain so far, but on the mountain, it'll be snow."

"My son is dressed in shorts."

"Mr. Nash, I'm sure Heather is taking care of your son."

"She's suffered a head injury, or did you forget that?"

"No, I'm aware of it, but our people are well trained and even if seriously injured, she's been trained to assist the survivor in all cases."

Lowering his eyes, Peter replied, "I'm sorry, but when this first happened, I expected Mike to be found and returned by dark. I don't mean to sound like I don't appreciate what you and your people are doing for us, because I do. I honestly do, but my wife and I are almost at our breaking points."

"I understand and most rescues are over within 48 yours, but this one has turned rough on us. One of the problems you and your wife have, if I may stick my nose in where I shouldn't, is you both need a lot of rest. Neither of you have slept for more than two or three hours a night, you're not eating properly, and I'd like to suggest you both see Doctor Patton."

Shaking his head, he replied, "I don't know if Wendy will see the doctor, but I'll ask. I know we're both worn out; worried about our son, tired, and eating very little. I've been living on caffeine since I got here."

John placed a hand on Peter's shoulder and said, "See the doc, let him give you both something to help you sleep and come back in the morning. Nothing will happen this day, believe me, not with a storm like this."

\*\*\*\*\*

Sitting with Wendy in his arms in front of the fireplace, Peter couldn't help but wonder about his son as he watched the flames dancing. *Lord, let Mike have a fire and allow Heather to help him survive. If she needs help, reach down with one hand, God, and assist her. I ask you to save both lives, Lord. Please, hear my cry for mercy. This I ask in the name of Jesus, amen.*

Wendy was asleep and her soft snores comforted Peter, so he took the pill Doctor Patton had given him and washed it down with a couple of sips of water. As we waited for the pill to work, tears suddenly formed in his eyes and a great shudder swept through his whole body, at just at the thought of losing his only son. Minutes later, his eyes and cheeks still wet, Peter Nash fell asleep on the sofa, his arms wrapped around Wendy.

A quarter after 4 am, Peter was up feeding his animals, but compared to most farmers and ranchers in the area, he didn't have many. However, he did have enough that he rose early to feed and care for them and besides, both Wendy and he were animal lovers. All animals on the place were treated more like their own children, than livestock. Clyde Wilkins had cared for the animals while they'd been at the Rescue Center and he had a small place less than a mile from the Nash place. Peter accepted the fact they were both up early, doing busy work, and it was a way to keep their minds off Mike, for a few minutes.

Entering the kitchen, once his chores were behind him, he moved to the coffee pot. Wendy neared and asked, "What's the weather look like?"

He shook his head and then said, "Cold and more snow would be my guess."

"Do we stay here or return to the Rescue Center?"

"We'll return. We may need to sleep here tonight, but there is no way I can sit here patiently with my child stuck on a snow-covered mountain."

"I'll get our coats."

As they moved over the snow-packed macadam road, Wendy wondered how anyone could survive in snow like this without a lot of gear. She looked at Peter and asked, "How can Mike still be alive in weather like this? I mean, to me, it looks like it would be impossible to live through one night."

"When I was in the army, we learned to survive in all kinds of weather and it's not as hard as it really looks, except survival doesn't mean comfort. By that I mean it's very likely Mike and Heather are hunkered down over a small fire trying to stay warm. They're both exhausted, injured, and hungry.""What do you think his chances really are, and don't tell me what you know I want to hear?"

Giving a dry chuckle, one that he hardly felt like giving, he replied, "I honestly think his chances are better now than when he was alone. I'm worried about the snakebite and the cold, but Mike is a tough little guy and there is nothing, absolutely nothing, that we can do to help him right now. I know Heather is well trained, so let's pray her injury is slight."

"I've prayed for her."

"I know you have, baby, and it's good we've brought God into this."

"Do you think this is God's way of maybe making us move closer to him? I mean, we're both believers, but there have been times we avoided church functions to do other things or failed to go at all because we wanted to just sleep in."

"Now, that is a question I don't feel qualified to answer. If it's us he's wanting to teach, then why is our son the one in danger? Momma always said, 'God works —"

"'In mysterious ways.' I've heard it a thousand times. I never really gave it much thought, until this happened. I'm so afraid of losing him."

"Now, stop. I want us both to try and keep our thoughts about Mike positive. He's no longer alone, last we heard he was alive, and we're going to get him as soon as this weather clears. I need you to be strong for me, because I'm having a hard time with this too. If we're both strong individually, then as a couple we'll be stronger as well, okay?"

Blinking back tears, Wendy gave a choked, "I . . . I'll try."

\*\*\*\*\*

John Smith stood in front of a long table in the welcome center, which had opened up for CAP use, and held a pointer in his right hand. He held a full cup of coffee with his other hand as he said, "Near dawn this morning, during a break in the snowstorm, a low flying private aircraft spotted smoke in this area. I've coordinated with all groups in the field and none have any members within a mile of the place. The location means Mike walked way off course and much further than we originally thought. Now, don't get your hopes up, especially you two, Peter and Wendy, because the smoke may not be Mike at all. Some people are known to camp in all kinds of weather, so we're not positive if it's hunters, trappers, hikers, or your son."

"Is there any way to check?" Peter asked.

"Yes, there is, but not immediately. I've asked the United States Air Force to send me a rescue chopper to check where the smoke was found, but the winds are too high right now. As soon as we have a break in the winds, I'll call and ask them to check the spot for us. They have agreed to take a look, so keep that in mind. Right now, none of my crews on the mountain can move, because the snow is too deep. I don't think any of us considered the need for snowshoes when we started this search."

"What about snowmobiles?" Peter asked.

Frank answered, "I asked the same question this mornin' and the problem is the winds. Some of the trails leadin' to where the smoke was spotted are narrow, Mr. Nash, and just one mistake could lead to additional injuries or deaths. Right now, she ain't an option, but who knows what noon will bring?"

"Frank is right and we've gathered the necessary resources, so now we play a waiting game. According to the weather folks, we'll have a short window of opportunity this afternoon, only it will be a short one, about two hours. I've contacted George Lee and his group, who are closest to the location and they'll give it a shot. Lee is using ATV's, because it would take too long to get a snowmobile up the side of the mountain and to the location. Another group that is close is Silas Hall, which most of you know, but he's afraid of a horse slipping and breaking a leg in this weather. He and Fred Bradley both volunteered to take their group and check on foot, but that's easier said than done. I think it'd take too long."

"Why can't the Air Force do the job?" Tom Pittman, a local trapper and hunter who'd just joined the group this morning, asked.

"According to their meteorologist, that area is a tricky place for winds, because it's a wide ravine and is known to have severe cross-currents of wind, whatever that means."

"Near as I can tell," Frank said, "and I talked to the weather lady, is it's like a river running into a larger river, but with rocks in the way. It causes the current of both rivers to run contrary to what a feller would expect, with all kinds of swirls and such."

John smiled and said, "So, we've got Silas and Fred's group on standby to move, just as soon as the weather guys and gals give me the okay. Any other questions?"

"What's the temperature and wind speed?" Peter asked.

"As of an hour ago, it was 18 degrees, with a wind gusting to 55 miles an hour."

"Good Lord," Peter said, "that's minus 8 degrees."

"Minus 6 actually, but you're close enough. Any other questions?"

*****

89

Mike stirred and opened his eyes. He felt some pain, but not nearly what he'd experienced the last time he'd woke up. He was able to bend his arm slightly, but the hand hurt when he tried to move it. He was freezing cold and then, with his heart filled with fear and hoping it had not burned out, he glanced toward the fire. Someone was bent over the flames, head drooping, and appeared to be asleep.

"Water?" Mike asked.

The head snapped up and Heather said, "I have some warm water right here. Now, I've been forcing it down you, so if you feel the need to pee, let me know and I'll turn my back. It's too cold for either of us to walk to the bushes."

"I don't think I could stand."

"You don't need to stand. Just roll over on your side and do your business. I'd introduce myself, only I don't know who I am."

"Huh?"

Giving a slight chuckle, the first in days, Heather said, "I'm part of a team mounted on ATV's that were looking for you, that is, if you're Mike Nash."

"I'm Mike, and I don't have to go yet."

"A couple of days back, I think it was, only I'm not sure, there was an earthquake and then an avalanche as a result. I have no idea what happened to my friends and I ended up in your camp, with my head bleeding and no memory to speak of, which is confusing."

"How do you remember the ATV's then?" Mike asked.

"That's a really good question, because I don't know. Seems parts of my memory has returned, but not all of it, and I get blinding headaches at times that almost make me want to cry."

"Migraines?"

"I really don't know, but think they might have to do with my injury. I've treated it and wrapped it, but I'm limited with what I can do out here. Are you feeling better?"

"Oh, yeah, only I'm not back to normal yet. Do you have any food?" Mike sat up and scooted his body closer to the flames of the fire.

"No, not a bite. I did go through your backpack looking for something to eat, and all I found were a few hard candies, a chocolate bar, and half a peanut butter sandwich."

"Good, can I have the sandwich? I'll share it with you?"

Heather glanced at him and said, "I fed it to you already, so it's gone. I've been nibbling on the chocolate."

"How long can we last without food?" Mike asked as he met her eyes.

"I honestly don't know the answer and hope we don't have to find out."

# CHAPTER *8*

"OKAY, folks, our window of opportunity for the rescue is closing quickly on us. I'm taking Frank and going to attempt to drop some food, clothing, and supplies to Mike's suspected location."

"Why doesn't the Air Force fetch them, I mean if you can fly to drop supplies?" Peter asked, knowing there was good reason.

John gave a dry laugh and replied, "Flight time from the base to here is too great. When our short window opens, for less than an hour, they'd not have time to get here, rescue the two, and then safely make it back. Oh, the crews are willing to try, but the commander, and wisely so, won't risk their lives."

"We have a small plane in the field below us and we're gonna fly over where the smoke was seen, circle a few times, then I'll throw the stuff out the side door." Frank said and then grinned.

John said, "It's all well packed and with international orange streamers, three feet long, attached to the canvas bags. I'll come in as low as I safely can, we'll drop the gear, then we'll have to return. One of the items packed will be a radio, so they can speak with us about their situation."

"What other gear is in the supplies, besides the radio? Is there some food?" Wendy asked.

"We've included arctic sleeping bags, a tent, three cases of military Meals Ready to Eat, or MRE's, and clothing items. The clothing items are either wool, Gortex, or Thinsolite, to help keep them warm if they get wet. Additionally, we've placed an EMT medical kit with the gear. This medical gear will allow Heather, if she can remember how to do the job, to treat both of them."

Doctor Patton spoke for the first time this morning, "The military rations have a high calorie count, which will help them keep warm. My biggest concern, obviously after the head injury and snakebite, is hypothermia and it's a disease that's easier to develop with limited food intake."

"I'm not sure what that is, doctor." Wendy said with a confused look on her face.

"Some call it the chills. There is a lot to the illness; it's not simple, but overall it means the inner core of a human body falls to an unsafe temperature level and it can lead to death. There are a number of stages, but everyone in this room has experienced the first stage, which is where we started shaking and shivering from cold weather. In the last stage, the victim becomes incoherent or irrational, and behaves in a bizarre manner. Victims are known to cast clothing aside, stumble, and behave almost as if intoxicated. Then comes unconsciousness, followed by death."

"Oh, my." Wendy said and then looked at Peter.

"One of the ways, doctor, the army taught me to prevent hypothermia was to drink hot fluids and to dress properly. They also stressed not over heating while working in cold weather."

"Yep," Patton replied, "and to suck hard candies. You were well trained to fight hypothermia."

"Two large bags of hard candies in the kits, Doctor Patton, so that's been thought of already. Are there any questions?" John said and then grinned.

Barbara stuck her head in the door and said, "John, weather just called and you have less than 30 minutes flight time to make your drop. Actually, the lady said 28 minutes."

"Let's go, Frank!" John said as he removed his coat from the rack.

Snow was still falling, but with huge lazy flakes that seemed to take forever to fall to the ground, and the wind was gone. John wasn't worried about the snow, but the wind could end up killing him and Frank. The mountains were a rough place for a small plane, with air pockets and currents that could mean a rough flight or even a crash. He'd survived a few crashes in the past and didn't relish the idea of doing so again. *A feller can only drop from the sky so many times and then his luck runs out,* he thought as he started removing 'removed before flight' pins and protective fabric covers from this small plane. The engine had a block heater, so he'd start quickly, unless there was another problem. He'd learned years ago that a cold engine could be impossible to start in arctic-like conditions.

Once in the cockpit, he ran down his check list with Joshua Boozer, his co-pilot. Joshua was a P. J. for the National Guard and pilot for CAP. They'd found his dual training helpful in more than one rescue attempt. Josh, as he was called, was of average size, well toned, and in top physical condition. John liked the man because he was intelligent and had a crazy humorous side. The PJ wore his auburn hair cropped short and was cleanly shaven. Like John and Frank, he was dressed in warm layers, in case they had to walk home.

Engine start and take off were uneventful and soon they were gaining altitude to approach the mountain. At times, as John turned the aircraft in slow 360's with the nose up to climb, a giant wind would cause the severe turbulence. As they flew, Josh was looking the map over.

"As cold as it is, they'll have a fire today too." Frank said over the intercom.

"Well, my biggest concern is not if they have a fire, but is either one of them in good enough condition to recover what we drop? I didn't bring it up in the meeting, because both the survivors and the folks waiting back at Rescue Center need something to believe in, and this will do the job. Besides, we have no idea they're not able to move, do we?"

"No and it's best to drop this stuff, so that they at least have a fightin' chance." Frank replied.

"I've got smoke on the hillside at your 1 o'clock position, almost straight ahead. Do you see it?"

"Roger on the smoke and I have a visual."

The aircraft dropped to about 50 feet above the trees and John buzzed the smoke four times, so the people on the ground could hear him. On the fifth pass over the smoke, Frank began pushing items out a small cargo door on the side. It took two passes to push all the gear out. As they left the area, John rocked the wings, which signaled he'd seen their smoke and knew where they were.

As he pulled the aircraft nose up to climb and gain altitude, the aircraft was shaken and buffeted by wind currents. "Help me with the yoke," John said to Josh.

Josh assisted and it was still difficult to hold the aircraft in position.

"Uh, I don't want to scare anyone, but we're getting' dang close to some trees on the left side of the aircraft." Frank said.

John glanced out his side window and prayed the forces of the wind would shift and they did, right at that instant. Suddenly, they were moving across smooth skies and John kept the aircraft below the cloud cover as much as possible. He'd known more than just a few pilots who'd flown in clouds and unexpectedly discovered a mountain top. Many survived, but a few died. His aircraft wasn't sophisticated with all kinds of black boxes, but rather a bare bones machine. He had no radar or other features fighter planes and more expensive personal planes carried. His bird was a working plane, no more and no less, stripped so it could carry gear or people.

"Frank, while dropping the stuff, did you see anyone?"

"No, not a soul. If both are hurt, it may take them some time to recover what we left for them."

"I hear that; now let's get back to camp and prepare to meet the press in a couple of hours. Be sure, Frank, to have a weather person on hand to explain the weather."

"I'll take care of it, boss."

*****

Right at the announced time, the press with their cameras were all positioned around the Rescue Center and snow was coming down harder now. Winds were strong enough to send white swirls of loose snow around like painted dust devils. John stepped to the microphone, gave his briefing and then turned it over to the weather representative.

Finally, Peter was motioned forward, so Wendy moved with him, and he cleared his throat before he said, "Uh, I want to thank John Smith and his whole team of professionals for the risks they've taken to get my son home safely. While Mike isn't home yet, it's not due to a lack of trying or pure guts. I also want all of us to remember those who were injured or killed on the night of the earthquake and keep their families in your prayers. I have every confidence that with the gear and supplies Heather and my son now have, they'll be able to wait out this storm in comfort."

A reporter called out, "How do you know your son is still alive, Mr. Nash?"

Giving an ill felt smile, Peter replied, "Dead people don't make campfires and keep them burning for days. Someone at that spot is alive and I pray it's both of them. If not, it's God's will."

Another reporter asked, "What's the first thing you intend to do when Mike is rescued, Mrs. Nash?"

Wendy smiled and replied, "Hug my son and then fix him his favorite meal."

"And what does he like to eat?"

---

"Pizza, and he'll have a large one for himself."

An older woman reporter raised her hand and asked, "Why haven't we heard from the parents of this Heather Edwards?"

John leaned toward the microphone and said, "Her father was a policeman and killed in the line of duty about five years ago. Her mother lives in Florida, so with the weather like it is, she's finding it hard to get here. As you all know, many flights have been canceled, leaving passengers stranded all over the United States. The last call I received from her she was in Kansas City and waiting. I have no other information at this time."

"Did she state how she felt about her daughter's situation?" the woman asked.

"No, she made no statements about her daughter, and I felt it would be inappropriate to ask. There are some things we in search and rescue do not need to ask and your question is one of them. Now, this concludes our daily briefing and we will answer no additional questions."

As Frank and John moved toward the trailer, Frank said, "That old heifer's pretty cold, ain't she? How does she think a person would feel with a child lost in the woods and knowing they've had a bad injury?"

John grinned and then said, "She's a reporter and don't you ever forget that. She is trained to write things so they sell papers, bring in viewers, or make money for the firm. I've met some good ones and I've met some of the other kind too. Her question was pretty typical and see, they use human emotions to attract folks. Did you read the paper the other day, after they spoke with the Nash family?"

"Nope, I don't read the daily rag."

"Well, the headlines read, 'State Search and Rescue Director NOT Worried about Dead,' which isn't an out and out lie. What I said was, I'm not worried about any dead, and I'm not. They will be recovered with both respect and dignity, and buried with full honors, but my job is to worry about survivors

—the living. Folks who have passed on have no pain and do not suffer. I have a young man and young woman on the side of that mountain, both in pain, and I will do what it takes to save them. I don't have time to worry about reporters, because I have a serious job to do."

"Well said, boss."

*****

Aunt Carol moved from the crowd near the reporters and approached Wendy. She smiled and then said, "Wendy, we're have a potluck meal here this evening and want you and Peter to join us. We don't think you need to be cooking at home and, well, after we eat, we thought we'd pray for Mike and Heather."

Peter, who was standing beside his wife said, "Aunt Carol, we sincerely appreciate the invitation, but I think it's going to have to be another time. Another front has moved in and we need to get home, shower, and relax before we turn in for the night. According to Mr. Smith, this weather will prevent any rescue efforts for at least three days."

Wendy met his eyes and he could tell he'd just said the wrong thing, so he said, "But, what do you think, dear?"

"Carol, we can't eat with y'all. While I appreciate the trouble you've all gone through, this publicity is rough on us, real rough, and we need some privacy. We will pray with all of you, if you can do it now. The roads are snowed over and we have animals to care for too."

"Well, let me go ask Janet, because it was her idea." Carol said and then walked off.

"Wendy, I realize they're family, but we need to get away from everyone for a while or I'm going to lose my mind at some point. I need just the two of us, alone, like last night."

"I agree, so we'll pray with them and then go home. How is that?"

*****

99

Mike was able to stand this morning, but his arm was sore and his movements were slow, like a very old man. The snow was knee-deep and the winds had picked back up. He was no longer hungry and moved to the flames to sip on some warm water.

He'd just sat by the flames when Heather, who'd just dropped a load of wood, said, "Do you hear that?"

"I hear something, but I don't know what it is." He turned his head in all directions.

"It's a gasoline engine of some sort. Listen, I think it's getting nearer."

"It is getting closer, but it's in the air, I think, or on a trail above us." Mike stood.

"I can't tell the direction!"

"It's right over us!"

"Something is wrong with my left ear, because I can't hear with it very well."

"Can you see the plane?" Mike asked.

"No, do you?"

"No, too many trees. Wait, I just saw something fall from the plane! I just saw a wing and side of a small airplane!"

"They must be dropping gear to us, because they can't pick us up in this weather."

Finally, Mike said, "They're leaving us."

"I can hear the engine but my ear must have been injured when I hurt my head. I can't tell any difference in the pitch of the engine."

"I can, and it's leaving. How do we get to the stuff they dropped?" Mike asked, grinning, because he suspected food and clothing.

"We need to plow our way through the snow to fetch it, because there is no other way. Can you walk?"

"I think so, but I can only carry or drag anything with one arm."

Patting him on the shoulder, she said, "I'll lead the way, but I can't move quickly. I've discovered if I move too fast, I get dizzy."

"No hurry, but I hope we don't lose anything they dropped to us."

Heather grew excited. "There may be a radio in the pack and if so, we'll get out of here eventually. Let's move and do it now." She moved toward the closest pack she could see, but after a few minutes she laughed and added, "This is a lot of work. I never would have guessed walking in snow could tire a person so quickly."

"We don't have any energy, 'cause we've not had much to eat."

"I think you could be correct. I sure hope there is some food in one of these bags."

Mike, his voice filled with excitement, said, "Off your left side is a bag that's closer to us."

Over the next hour, they'd recovered four of the five bags dropped, and now they sat grinning beside the fire. The last bag had bounced down a deep ravine and they could not reach it, due to all the snow. Heather noticed each bag was marked with what looked like the contents. She pulled the one marked food to her side and opened it.

"There is food in this bag, Mike! But, we can only eat a little bit since we've been without food for a few days. If we eat too much we'll throw up or could even die, I think."

"Oh, I'm so hungry." the boy said.

"Here's a food pouch for you and one for me. I'm not sure why I remember it, but these are called MRE's and they're a complete meal in a plastic bag. After you open the bag, you'll see a smaller bag marked entree. Eat about half of it and then stop, okay?" Heather said as she handed an MRE to Mike. She was all smiles and felt as if a great disaster had been averted with the simple drop of the bags.

They both ate slowly as only hungry people do, enjoying the texture of the food, the taste and the juices. Unlike the movies, where the hungry gobble their food down, Mike realized he wanted to take his time and enjoy his first meal in days. His arm was still swollen, but the deep hurting was gone. Some pain remained, but usually only when he attempted to use his hand, so he was eating with his left hand now.

As she ate, Heather began going through the other bags. She squealed and giggled like a little girl at Christmas time, because she pulled out clothing, a tent, sleeping bags, cooking gear, a pistol, and a folding 30.06 rifle, along with a box of shells for each. The clothing was their sizes and had been packed especially for them. Handing long trousers, a wool shirt and heavy coat to Mike she said, "Put these on and do it now. You'll be a lot warmer with this stuff on, but strip down to your underwear and place your old clothing aside. I'll turn my back, so change."

Mike quickly changed and moaned with the instant increase of heat and said, "You change now, because it's a lot warmer."

Snow was still falling, but the winds were milder, so once changed, Heather started on the tent. It took her four times longer than normal, because she often forgot what she was doing or what she was supposed to do next. It was frustrating to her, but once the tent was up, she placed all the personal gear in the tent, along with the sleeping bags. She left out the weapons, cooking and signaling gear, as well as two wool blankets. The blankets would keep them warm tonight as they sat by the small fire.

"If they know where we are," Mike asked, "why didn't they rescue us?"

"I don't know. I think, but don't really know, we have some bad weather coming. That's why I got the tent up and our gear stored inside. I think they packed a radio in a bag, but it must be the one at the bottom of the gorge. With the snow like it is, we'll not be able to recover it."

"They'll come, because they've located us now."

"Yep, they'll come." she said and then thought, *but I hope we're both still alive when they get here.*

# CHAPTER 9

MEANWHILE, back at the Rescue Center, Barbara said, "I've been trying to reach Heather for hours, but no response. Do you think the radio was damaged when the bag struck the ground?"

"Anything is possible, but keep trying off and one throughout the night. We're not even sure they were able to recover a single bag. The winds were too tricky to hang around and we barely escaped as it was."

"Well, let's pray they were at least able to recover the food and clothing items, or it'll be rough on them. Weather is calling for an additional 12 to 14 inches of snow in the mountains by morning, with temperatures well below freezing."

"We've done all we can for them and they'll have to make it with what they have on hand. Any bags not recovered will be covered with snow, and soon, too."

Frank stuck his head in the door and said, "I have about a dozen more volunteers that just showed up, so do ya want me to put 'em with the others?" The volunteers were being housed in a huge warehouse next to the visitor's center that was normally used to store recreational park vehicles during the off season.

"That'll be fine, and get with Tom Johnson to add all the names to our listing of volunteers. Make sure he allows for feeding and bedding of an additional dozen folks."

"I'll see he knows, boss." Frank said, and then closed the door.

Peter neared and asked, "Do you think they may have retrieved the bags dropped to them?"

"Mr. Nash, I honestly don't know and have no way of knowing. Both of them are seriously injured, the bags are heavy, and then they'd have to bust snow to get to each bag. No, I don't think they have all of them, or we'd have received some communications from them by now."

"How does cold weather impact the batteries?"

"In super cold weather, like we have now, the battery life is shorter, but Heather has been trained to keep the batteries warm. I don't think it's a battery issue, but it could be. I honestly think they were either too weak to move the bags, or they only found some of them."

"Let's hope and pray they found the bags containing food and clothing."

"That'd be enough to keep them alive, for sure, if they have a good shelter constructed and they stay out of the wind. I don't want to sound all negative, because I'm not. Both Heather and Mike have their acts together in the woods and I fully expect to rescue both of them alive, as soon as this front moves on."

"I don't know if my wife and I can take much more of this waiting. All she does is cry and pray."

"Patience is needed in rescue, but crying isn't hurting her any and I think praying may help us a great deal. No one I know in rescue is against a little or lot of help from God, if the situation calls for it and this one clearly does."

The main door of the trailer opened and a woman walked in wearing a parka, but as soon as the hood dropped, John knew the woman.

"Well, Sandy, I see you finally got here. I would ask about the flight, but I've already heard on the news. Wait a minute, if the flights have been canceled, how did you get here?" John asked.

Sandy laughed and said, "I got mad, rented a car and drove here. I wouldn't be much of a mother, if I didn't care enough about my daughter to make the trip."

Sandy looked enough like Heather to be her sister instead of her mother. They were both about the same size, same color hair and shapely. While Heather was a tomboy, Sandy was a first-class woman and she looked the part, as well.

"Sandy, meet Mr. Peter Nash. Mike is his son and he's the boy with your daughter. Did you get my text messages?"

As Sandy and Peter shook hands, she said "Yes, and the last I got was about twenty minutes ago, stating the weather was still rough."

"Good, then you're current on all we know."

"So, now we wait?" she asked.

"Yes, the area near the front door is for y'all to relax and we have two bedrooms down the hall. On the counter you'll find coffee or hot water for tea. Soft drinks and milk in the fridge. We have one rule here, no alcohol of any kind, and anyone caught drinking will be escorted off the park. Any questions?"

"No, none I can think of."

"Good, now I want you and Peter both to go to the living room so we can get some work done."

\*\*\*\*\*

Silas looked around his camp and shook his head. It was freezing cold and his folks were uncomfortable, even with the gear they had with them. He'd been informed by radio of the drop and knew there was a good chance the survivors recovered some of the bags. He also knew from experience it was hard to recover all dropped gear and this snow would swallow a bag, leaving no sign of being there, especially with the wind covering all traces. He'd heard nothing about Heather contacting them, so he was sure they hadn't found the communications bag.

"What are you thinking on so seriously over there, boss?" Ben asked.

"I was wondering what gear the survivors may have recovered."

"I don't think it matters much to them, because it'll seem like a birthday and Christmas all rolled up into one for them. They need clothing and food, so let's pray they got that much."

"I was thinking about a radio."

Ben shrugged and replied, "It won't help 'em much. By now the boy is either dead or alive from the snakebite and it's the same with Heather and her head injury. A radio won't help them get rescued any quicker, so I don't see it as a big deal."

Silas laughed and said, "Strange way to look at it, but I guess you're right. It'd just be good to know if they're in good or sad shape, ya know?"

"It's a luxury, boss, nothing more and nothing less. It will help the rescue team, but as for assisting them in survival, not a player. Heather knows as much as any man here about survival, so your radio would only confirm their medical conditions."

"I hear ya." Silas replied and then said, "Oliver, I want you and a couple of the boys to put a windbreak up around the horses. This weather keeps up like it is and we'll start losing animals."

"I hear ya, pa. Come on, Lewis and Ed, give me a hand." Oliver stood and made her way to the supplies, where she pulled out a couple of tarps.

"P.W., put some coffee on, son, and make yourself useful." Silas said with a smile.

At 16, Phillip Wadsworth Hampton was the youngest member of the group, and he was more or less along for the ride, to see if rescue interested him or not. He moved to the fire and opened the coffee pot. A minute later he said, "Do you know there is a sock in this pot?"

"Yep, but it's clean or is supposed to be. Just untie 'er, empty the thing, and fill it with grounds."

"How much is too much coffee?"

Silas laughed and when he sobered, he winked and replied, "Son, if you can float a horseshoe in it, it's perfect. A cowboy or cowgirl will drink any strength of coffee, just as long as it's hot. I do have to warn ya though, the stronger the better in their eyes."

Ten minutes later, sitting beside a perking coffee pot, Silas smiled when Oliver neared and sat on a log they used as a sofa. As he looked at her face, his smile disappeared and he asked, "Problem with the horses?"

"Now, and I don't like telling you this, but Lewis lost his gloves a while back and I think his fingers have frostbite."

"Lewis! Get over here, son, and do the job now!"

"I'm comin', pa!" Lewis called out from his tent.

When he neared the fire, he glanced at Oliver and said, "Thanks for squealing on me, sis."

"Leave her alone and let me take a look at your hands." Silas said, hoping the fingers were just red.

"They're okay, or will be as soon as they warm up." Lewis extended both hands toward the fire.

"They've white patches on them, son, and that's a sign of frostbite. Why didn't you tell me of this before?"

"Warm 'em up and I'll be ready to go."

"Lewis, listen to me son, they're injured and seriously. I'm going to warm 'em up, but ya won't like me doin' the job, not one bit."

"Are you sure? They don't hurt."

Alfred, quiet as usual, suddenly said, "Lewis, trust your father on this; you may even lose a finger or two on each hand. I've seen a lot of frostnip or frostbite, it's the same injury, during my lifetime, and you're in trouble right now."

"From cold hands?" Lewis asked in disbelief.

"Yep, the tissue is frozen and damaged."

Silas said, "P.W., get me a pot of water and place it on the fire. Heat it to lukewarm and no hotter."

Apprehensive, Lewis asked, "W . . . what are you going to do?"

"We have to warm the frozen tissue slowly to avoid any additional damage. How'd this happen, son?"

Last night, on my shift of guard, I lost my gloves and I've been without them since. Pa, do you mean to sit there and tell me I might lose fingers over this?"

Meeting his son's eyes, Silas said, "I'm dead serious, Lewis. How cold is it out here, son? Fifteen below, maybe?"

"Close to that."

"Once away from this fire, how long before all exposed flesh will freeze? Minutes, maybe?"

"Okay, pa, I see what you mean. I didn't think it was a big deal and I didn't want to be a complainer."

"Next time, if there is a next time, wear your gloves. If you lose them, report it immediately, do you understand? I'm about to cause you some terrible pain and do you know what? It's all preventable and you'd better hope the treatment works, or Edward will be sawing black fingers off."

"My fingers aren't black."

110

"No, they're not right this minute, but if this treatment doesn't work, they'll soon turn that color."

"My God, pa!"

"This water is warm to the touch now, Mr. Hall." P. W. said and then gave a worried look.

Silas moved to the pot and pulled it from the hot coals. He met his son's eyes and said, "Come on, Lewis, the sooner we get you fixed up the less damage you'll have in the long run."

Lewis, now understanding the seriousness of his injury moved to his father's side and said, "Do what it takes and don't worry about me."

"Son, I'm going to place your hands in this pot of warm water for a long time. Once done, we'll gently dry 'em off, and then warm 'em up. This is going to hurt you, but it's the only way to treat your injury that I know of in the field."

When Lewis' hand entered the water, he gave a loud gasp and his feet began kicking at the snow. He never expected the level of pain simple warm water brought him. Tears rolled down his cheeks as he jerked and twitched, but he remained by the fire.

Many long minutes later, Silas removed his son's hands from the water and softly dried them. Lewis' eyes were rimmed in red and tears were still seen on his cheeks. He sniffled and said, "That was rough. How long before I know if I'll lose any fingers or not?"

"Two or three days and you'll know." Fred spoke again and then added, "But, if they have to come off, we'll have to do the job here, most likely. This storm is nowhere near blown out and it might be a week before help could reach us. By then, it'd be wasted effort."

"Here?" Lewis asked, his face pale.

"Relax, my friend," Ben said, "I can do the job and I even have some medication to help kill the pain a little. I just hope you've learned something from all of this."

"I . . . I have. I didn't want to complain over something as trivial as gloves."

"Just like pa. You're hard-headed." Oliver said, then met her daddy's eyes and smiled.

"Son, get some sleep. Warming those hands hurt you and I know it. In the future, keep them both warm and covered, or they'll freeze faster the next time."

"Really?" Lewis asked, not sure if pa was being serious or pulling his leg.

"Really, and remember it; now off to bed." Silas said as he thought, *I hope we don't have to remove his fingers, or there will be hell to pay around here. I think all Ben has is a local for pain and that just won't be strong enough to do the job.*

After Lewis went to bed, Oliver asked, "Pa, what are the chances of his fingers being removed?"

"About 50-50, and its serious business. If the weather was better, I'd send him to a hospital and do it now. But, to be honest, they'd not be able to do much more that what we did. See, the tissue has been damaged and only time will tell how much."

The wind picked up, sending little white devils whirling around the camp and Silas thought they resembled miniature tornadoes. With the wind up and temperature down, he was worried about the horses, windbreak or no. To him, horses were special and he didn't have a one he didn't love deeply and spoil. While a hard man in many ways, he had a soft spot for all women and horses and knew it, so he played tough all the time. Most of the time, Oliver saw right through his act.

His wife died of breast cancer years ago and he'd never remarried. He didn't like bars, didn't socialize much, and at church all the women his age were married, so he'd remained single. He liked women and grew lonely at times, but working a ranch kept him busy and he had little time for emotions that were self-centered. He'd only met one woman in the ten years since his wife's death and she tried to change him, something he'd never allow to happen. Besides, she'd not been a country gal and loved the big city lights. As far as Silas was concerned, he'd left nothing in any big city he needed to fetch. He knew if a woman was intended for his life, God would send her to him.

He picked up the radio, knowing it was monitored around the clock and said, "Rescue Center, this is Cowboy One, over."

After a second or two the radio came alive, "Go Cowboy One."

"Be advised we have a man down with frostbite. His name first name is lima, echo, whiskey, India, Sahara. Last name is hotel, alpha, lima, lima. Do you copy?"

"Roger that, Lewis Hall."

"Correct. The injury is to both hands, repeat, both hands and severe."

"Understand both hands. Be advised, medical evacuation is impossible at this time." Rescue Center immediately replied.

"My Medic is monitoring his condition. He has been treated and will be watched closely over the next few days."

"Copy. The weather folks are predicting another front that is right behind this one. There may be a small window of opportunity where we can get your man out."

"Understand. We are capable of treating the injury, but lack painkillers."

"If we're unable to remove your man, we may be able to drop you supplies." Center replied and then static filled the radio for a few seconds.

"Roger that and nothing we can do now but wait."

"Anything else to report?"

"Colder than a well diggers left leg out here, but we're well equipped. We have about fourteen inches of snow, high gusting winds, and my last reading showed minus fifteen ambient air temperature."

"Better you than me, Cowboy." the voice at Rescue Center said.

Giving a light chuckle, Silas replied, "Cowboys are tough. Anything else we need to be aware of at this time?"

"Negative. All operations have ceased to wait out the storm. Hunker down, Cowboy."

"Will do, Center. Cowboy One, out."

Ben, was sitting on the log and said, "Silas, I can remove the fingers, but Lewis won't like it much if all I have is a local anesthesia."

"How quickly can you remove one?"

"Easily in less than a minute, but that doesn't count cleaning each finger and bandaging them."

Staring at the fire, the old rancher said, "I hope my boy keeps all his fingers, only we'll do what we have to do to keep him alive. It'd hurt me to see his fingers cut off, but life is full of difficulties and we won't have a choice if they turn black."

"Silas, you and I have been friends for how long, maybe twenty-five years?"

"About that, why?"

"Have you even known me to sugar-coat horse apples and call 'em candy?"

"No, my friend, you've always been open and blunt, but I like that trait in you. I don't think you could be politically correct if you wanted to do the job, which I know you don't."

"I'll be honest with you dealing with Lewis, but remember, it'll be me the trained EMT talkin' and not me, the cowboy talkin'. I can't lie to you, so I may say something you'll not like."

"Son, as long as you're up and up with me, I can face reality."

Gazing into the older man's eyes, Ben said, "Remember what you just said. No matter what I tell you, you can face reality, and I'm going to hold you to that. See, there is a chance Lewis may lose a hand or both, depending on the depth of tissue damage. Only time will tell the exact extent of his injuries."

Silas took a drink of his coffee, thought for a minute, and then said, "Oh, Jesus, I hope not. It'd kill him to lose both of his hands."

Ben nodded, lowered his head, and looked at his now cold coffee cup in his hands.

# CHAPTER 10

HEATHER stood at the top of the gorge and wonder how she could get down the sides, collect the bag, and then get back up again. She didn't seem to feel the cold and stood with her mitten covered hands on her hips, studying the situation. *There must be a way,* she thought as she turned and then moved toward the fire. *I just need to think this out carefully or one slip and I'm dead.*

Back at the fire, she sat on a log, pushed the hood of her parka back and gave thought to the bag. *The only item she really wanted in the bag was a radio, maybe, but she had no real idea what it contained. Even if it has a radio, what good will it do me right now? Nothing can fly in this weather, the storm seems to be lasting forever, and both of us can live with our injuries. We have food, water, shelter and a fire, so is a radio worth the risk?* she wondered and then threw another log on the fire.

"What are you thinking about?" Mike asked.

"If I should attempt to get the bag in the gorge."

"What do you think is in it worth the danger?"

She looked at him, met his eyes and replied, "A radio, I think."

"Think? You mean you don't know?"

"I'm really not sure if they dropped a radio at all, but I suspect they did." She broke eye contact with him and stared at the dancing flames.

"I don't think it's worth getting hurt or killed, if we don't know what is in the thing. I mean, they can't get us out during this storm or they'd be here, right?"

"It's the winds, I think. If the winds are too high it's dangerous for helicopters and planes."

"Well," Mike said and then grew quiet, but finally said, "they'll not walk here unless they've some long legs. There must be over 16 inches of snow on the ground and just breaking through snow to get bags almost wore you out."

"No, we'll not be rescued by anyone on foot. I suspect snowmobiles, but that'll have to wait for this storm to die. They need to be able to read a map, determine their location and see how to drive. As hard as this snow is falling right now, it'll be a while."

"Couldn't they use a GPS?"

"Maybe, but I'm no expert on them. I know in my car, if the weather is bad the GPS sometimes doesn't work well. I honestly don't know."

"We've got a tent, sleeping bags, and food, so we can wait. I don't like it, because I suspect I'm in trouble when I get home, but we'll survive."

"What about the radio?"

"I say we wait for the weather to get better and then find an easier way into the gorge, if we need to get the bag. Right now, with the weather like it is, and you already said they can't come and get us, the radio is nothin' we need. I don't think we should take a chance of one or both of us getting hurt anymore. If they knew where to drop the bags, they must already know where we are, don't you think?"

Suddenly, Heather grabbed her head and screamed as a sudden flash of pain cut through the middle of her head. She fell backward, off the log, and began to jerk and twitch.

Mike, thinking she was dying, ran to her side, but with her moving so violently he dared not get too close. He stayed just outside the reach of her flying arms and legs. As her movements became more vicious, he became frightened that he'd be left alone, and with a dead person. He kept his eyes open as he watched her limbs flailing and prayed.

Minutes later, her movements slowed and then came to a complete stop.

"Heather?" Mike asked, hoping she wasn't dead.

"I'm . . . I'm okay. I had a . . . seizure of . . . some sort."

"You scared me."

"I'm fine now, if you'll help me . . . get up. I'm very weak."

"Does your head still hurt?"

"No, not now, not like it did." Mike helped her gain her feet and then move to the log. Once sitting, she added, "It felt like a knife blade was being forced in my brain."

His eyes huge, Mike replied, "You screamed before you fell and I thought you were dying. Don't die on me, please, because I'm scared of dead people."

Giving a light chuckle, she said, "Mike, dead people can't hurt you, only those alive can harm people. I'd try to help you, even if I were a ghost." *The last thing I need to do is die with this young man, because he needs help,* she thought.

"Please, don't talk about death and ghosts; I don't like it."

"Okay, I won't. Only, if something does happen to me, now I'm not saying it will, but if it does, just pull my body closer to the trail and pray for me. I'm not scared of death, but since you don't want to talk about it, we won't. How's the arm?"

"I don't have as much swelling, but my fingers are still numb, some of them anyway, and it hurts when I use my hand."

"I'm not a medic, but I think once all the swelling goes down and you've time to recover, the hand will stop hurting."

"I sure hope so." He sat quietly for a while watching the snow fall and then asked, "Do you think I'll get in trouble when I get home?  I mean, you told me a lot of folks are out looking for me."

"Trouble?  I don't think so.  Why would you be in trouble?"

"I broke a big rule in scouting.  I was to tell one of the adults before I left the others and I didn't." he replied and then thought, *Mr. Bailey and Mr. Banks both told us a number of times to never just walk off.  They'll be mad for sure.*

"Well, the scouts might want to talk to you about that, but I think your mom and dad will be happy to have you home. But, no matter what happens, you have to handle it like a man and not a child."

"What do you mean?"

"It won't be long and you'll be a man.  You've just survived some pretty rough weather and I think you've done a lot of growing up in the last few days. Not many men could have done what you did and still be alive.  I honestly think, well, most would have died."

"I prayed a lot and knew pretty much what I had to do, thanks to the Scouts. The hardest part was trusting God and being alone."

"That trusting God was hard, huh?"

"After the snake bite, I tried to pray and make sense, but I was scared, in pain, and not sure He understood what I was saying.  I'm not even sure I understood what I was saying."

"I think He knew, because He knows our hearts and minds. He knew you needed help, so He sent me to help."

"I'm glad you're with me, but sorry you got hurt. I worry about your head, because the jerking and flopping on the ground scares me. I want to help you, but don't know how."

"I don't think there is anything you can do to help me. We'll be rescued as soon as the weather breaks and I'll go to a hospital."

"W . . . will I have to go too?"

"I think it'd be smart to have a doctor look at you, don't you agree?"

"Yeah, I think so, but I don't like doctors much."

Heather smiled and then asked, "Is it because of shots?"

Lowering his head, he replied, "How did you know?"

"I used to feel the same about doctors when I was about your age. As you get older, you see a reason for the immunizations and understand how they help keep us alive."

"I guess they're needed, but I still don't like 'em."

Heather gave a light laugh and said, "Let's air out our sleeping bags near the tent. Use the low limb that hangs over the log and only for an hour or so. Tomorrow, if is a little warmer, I'll heat up some water and we'll take turns wiping ourselves down. Neither of us has had a bath in days."

"We'll have to do that beside the fire, huh?"

"For sure and you'll need to wipe your whole body, not just your face and hands. There is a small bar of soap in the supplies. That means the other will have to either leave camp for a few minutes or turn their back if they stay near the fire."

"Okay, but it'll be cold."

Heather moved the rifle that was in the gear to the other side of the log and then fetched her sleeping bag and Mike's. She had him hold one sleeping bag, as she threw the other over the limb. Taking the second bag, she repeated the process.

"They are getting gamey." she said and then moved to the fire.

The rest of the day was spent checking the shelter, gathering wood, and inventorying supplies. The bags had a lot of different gear and she'd found water purification tablets, two first aid kits, wool socks and clothing, all sized to fit her and Mike. She had him change into dry socks and set the clothing aside.

Then she said, "I have clean clothing here, so tomorrow after we wash, we can get into them. I'm sure we'll both smell better after a scrub down."

Mike asked, "When can we eat?"

"Are you hungry?" Heather teased, knowing boys his age were always hungry.

"Yep and I like those MRE's."

"We have two and a half cases of those, so take two meals out tonight and you can eat both."

Mike began digging in a bag and then said, "Beef ravioli sounds good and I'll make the other, uh, buffalo chicken. I might not be able to eat both meals, but what I don't eat, I'll have in the morning for breakfast."

After he opened both meal bags, Heather asked, "What's all in yours? I have a pork rib, potato soup, energy bar, and cheese spread."

The chicken has rice and beans, turkey nuggets, and cookies. I love cookies, too."

"And, in the other?"

Mike cut it open and said, "Cheese spread, toaster pastry, crackers and an orange drink. I have coffee, but I don't drink it, so do you want it to drink?"

"Sure, I'll take it."

"I have apple cider too, and that'll be good hot."

"These meals taste flat to me, even warmed up, don't you think?"

"They're okay, but not as good as my mom's cooking."

Heather laughed and replied, "I'd guess not. Moms are the best cooks in the world, don't you think?"

"I don't want to talk about moms or dads, because it makes me sad. I know mom is scared and upset that I'm out here. I don't like the thought I have hurt my mom and have her worried."

"I think she's more worried than upset with you. You're not in trouble, so let that slide from your mind. Your mother and father love you and they want you back home safe."

Mike nodded but remained quiet as he ate.

An hour late, the meal finished, Heather had just added a log to the fire when she heard a noise from the woods to their left. It was something moving in the snow and it sounded like a rescue party or a group of men. It was well past full dark now and while the snow had stopped, the wind gusts were strong.

"W —what was that noise?" Mike asked as he moved closer to her on the log.

"I'm unsure, but whatever it is, it's big."

"Do, uh, do you think it might be someone looking for us?"

"They'd have called out by now, because the flames from our fire would be easy to see." she said and then thought, *I hope it's not a bear or a moose.*

She pulled the 30.06 rifle up, chambered a round, and waited.

Long minutes went by and she finally spotted movement. It was brown in color, was all she could tell by the dim light of the fire. She flicked the safety off and waited. As she sat, she could hear her heart beating loudly in her chest and prayed it wasn't a bear. Eventually, she thought, *it'll either come closer or move away. Please, God, make it go away, because I don't want to have kill to stay safe.*

"My, uh, my Scout Master said there were bears in these mountains." As Mike spoke she could hear the fear in the young man's voice. He pulled a whistle from his pocket and said, "I was told to blow my whistle, if I saw a bear. I think it scares them."

"What else did he teach you about bears? Now, I'm not sure that's what's out there, but it's either that or a moose. Moose can be as mean as a bear, depending on how they're feeling at the moment."

"Why don't you shoot one shot into the air and when you finish, I'll blow the whistle?"

"Okay, let me know when you're ready." Heather knew bears usually left people alone, only she honestly knew little about them.

"I'm ready, so when —"

Suddenly Heather heard something running toward them from the brush. It was big because the noise was loud, louder than any human could have been. Suddenly, snow fell from brush almost in camp, limbs were heard to snap, and a large bear stood on his rear legs and sniffed the air. Finally smelling them, he dropped to all fours and gave a loud growl.

Heather, sensing Mike was ready to run, whispered, "Don't move or it will kill us." Her finger was firmly against the trigger and she hoped she didn't have to kill the big animal. *If he takes one step closer or charges, I'll have to shoot. I'll fire a warning first and then shoot to kill, need be,* she thought.

The young animal growled and then saliva dripped from the long sharp teeth when his mouth opened a second later to roar. The animal watched both of the humans closely, looking for the slightest movement or threat. Finally, the bear turned and moved toward the woods, but Mike moved and the big beast spun completely around and looked at the two again, as if undecided.

Heather sighted the animal in as she thought, *please go away. I don't want to shoot you, so help me, but I will to protect us.*

The bear took a step forward, Heather's rifle sounded with a loud *boom*, and the whistle in Mike's mouth began making a loud nonstop piercing noise. Her shot had flown by the head of the bear closely and he suddenly remembered the smell that brought him here. Each time he'd smelled this scent, he'd heard this same loud noise, and more than once he'd felt a deep pain. Humans! He quickly turned tail and fled deeper into the mountain, wanting nothing more to do with this camp or the people living there.

When the bear took off running, Heather stood and squeezed off another round, which struck the snow-covered ground right behind him. Since it was dark and snowing, she didn't see the bear's speed increased a great deal.

Mike stood and watched the direction the bear had run, no longer scared. He could hear brush being knocked out of the way as it moved away from him. His deep fear and tension immediately left him.

"W . . . will he . . . come back?" Mike asked as he met Heather's eyes.

"I have no idea, but we scared him pretty good. I'm no expert on bears, but if he does come back, I don't think it will be tonight. The next time we encounter a bear, if we do, don't run, because they'll think you are prey and attack you."

"I was scared and wanted to run to get away."

"You can't outrun him, even if we didn't have all this snow. I read someplace that a bear can outrun a horse for short distances, so if he returns, have your whistle ready and I'll shoot to kill. I've never killed a bear before, but I've heard they don't die easily."

"I was about to go to sleep, but no way now."

"Make and drink your apple cider and let your blood pressure drop. That big beast scared both of us and it should; it's a dangerous animal in the wild like this."

As Mike prepared his water to boil, she noticed his hands shaking, and turning away from him, she held her hands out. Hers were trembling as well.

# CHAPTER 11

LATE the next day, two fingers on Lewis' hand were black and swollen. He glanced at his fingers, his dad, and then finally at Benjamin. "These will have to come off, huh?"

"Yep, they will, and the medication I have won't kill all the pain either."

"When, uh, do they need to be removed?"

"Directly would be best." Ben said and then winking at Lewis he continued, "I have some whiskey to kill the pain, if you want it."

"No, we don't drink, so I'll pass on the booze. Have you ever done this before?"

"Huh-uh, except I know how it's done. It looks like both need to come off at the second knuckle of each finger and that'll be easy to remove. The problem, seriously, will be your pain."

"I'll deal with the pain, but how long will it take?"

"I think about a minute a finger. Can you handle that?"

"Sure, I guess."

"When we're done, I'll give you something to help you sleep. And, before you ask, it'd not put you into a deep sleep, so I can't give it to you to help with your pain. It's whiskey or nothing."

"Nothing. Whiskey is good for no person. I'll handle the pain, but you do it right the first time, okay?"

"I hear you. Let me get my supplies to boiling in some water, so relax a while. It'll be a good half hour before we start anything." Bob began gathering what he'd need to complete the removal of the two blackened fingers.

Thirty minutes later, Bob said, "Silas, I want you to sit on his chest and Alfred, you hold his injured hand steady. He'll not feel much until I get almost to the bone, then he'll go nuts on us. No matter what he does, Alfred, you have to keep his hand still or I might just take off the wrong finger. Oliver, fetch me a limb around two inches in diameter and maybe a foot long. He can bite on that as I do the doctoring."

Since Ed was the unofficial medic, he asked, "What do you have to prevent post surgery infection?"

"I thought to initially use alcohol and then apply a triple antibiotic on the stubs three times a day. Think that will work?"

"Oh, yea, and he'll just have to keep the hand clean. I'm sure glad you're doin' this and not me. I honestly don't think I could cut on a man like this."

"Ed," Silas said, "I'd do the job, need be, because the only other choice is to allow him to die of infection. He's my son, and while I don't want to hurt him, by golly, I'd do it to save his life."

"Oh, I didn't mean I couldn't do it. I meant I wouldn't like doin' the job."

Oliver returned with the wood and when she handed it to Ben, he said, "Build the fire up and keep it burning high, because it'll be dark soon. I'll need light to do the amputations."

A few short minutes later, Ben said, "Here, bite on this limb and remember, if you want a drink of whiskey, just let me know. Now, extend the arm and let me give you a local to kill the pain a bit."

Taking the wood in his good hand, Lewis said, "No whiskey, and I meant it. You worry about the cutting and I'll handle the pain." He then placed the limb in his mouth and extended his hand.

Once the local was given, Ben waited. As he waited, he removed his scalpel from the boiling water and placed it on some sterilized gauze.

He then said, "Ed, when I need something, I'll need it quickly, so hand it to me as soon as you can. He'll bleed like a stuck hog with both fingers off, so I'll need the whiskey first and then the antibiotic ointment next."

"I hear ya." Ed said and pulled cork from the whiskey bottle.

"If you're ready, Lewis, nod." Ben said.

Lewis nodded and Ben picked up the scalpel and turned his back to his patient, so he couldn't see what was being done. He selected the worst looking finger and quickly ran the razor sharp blade completely around the ruined finger.

Lewis grunted; he bit into the wood so hard he was shivering, and his body gave small jerks.

Blood, with its strong coppery smell, began to run from the finger, as Ben cut a few tendons and then twisted the finger to allow easier access. Less than a minute after starting, the finger fell to the dirt near the fire.

"How are you hangin', Lewis?" Silas asked from his son's side.

Pulling the wood from his mouth, he replied, "It's . . . it's rough . . . dad. Is . . . he . . . done?"

Giving a dry laugh, which he surely didn't feel, Silas said, "One down and one to go. Pray, son, and God will lessen your pain. I'd rather have this done to me than you, boy, but I can't."

"I've got the bleeding under control now, Lewis, so relax, put the stick back in your mouth and let's finish this job."

The second finger was his middle finger and Ben found the tendons harder to reach as he cut and Lewis was about insane from the pain. Suddenly the stick fell from his mouth, he gave a sigh and his head fell back.

"Is he dead?" Silas asked. *Lord, please, don't take my son,* he thought.

"No, he's fine, but the pain was too much, so he's passed out. This boy of yours, well, he's got grit and is one tough man." Ben replied and then watched the middle finger join the other one in the dirt.

Blood spurted high into the air as Alfred let go of the hand, turned and puked, and then said, "Sorry, Ben, but this gets to me." He wiped his mouth off with the back of his hand.

Silas, seeing the crimson on the gauze asked, "Should the blood leak on the pads like that? I mean, it seems like a lot of blood."

"Uh-huh, it's normal. Now that the fingers are gone, I'll pour some alcohol on them and once it dries, I'll apply some triple antibiotic on the stubs. They'll both drip blood as I do this, so don't freak out on me. Unless he gets infected, he'll be as good as new in a few weeks."

Silas extended his hand toward Ben and said, "I want to thank you for saving my son's life."

*Dang,* thought Ben, *he's serious,* but said, "I didn't really save his life, because I think we'll be out of here before his injury would have been life threatening. But the fingers needed removing, so I did the job." He then took the hand of his boss.

As they shook, Ben saw tears in the eyes of Silas. As the first tear fell, Ben said, "This wood smoke sure gets to a feller's eyes, doesn't it?"

Silas laughed and when sober he said, "Yes, it always makes me cry. But, Ben, I owe you one."

"Get out of here, and you owe me nothin'. Ain't a man here who wouldn't do what it takes to help any of us and you know it, too. Besides, we don't know if he'll survive my surgery or not."

"Your words ring true, but you're the only one who picked up the scalpel, my friend."

"Shouldn't you call base and let them know of Lewis' condition?" Ben asked, wanting to keep the man from losing control of his emotions again.

Silas called the Rescue Center, explained about Lewis and then said, "Copy, I understand. No, all of our horses are fine. Will do. Roger that. Over and out." He placed the radio back in his coat pocket.

"Well?" asked Oliver, her eyes wide.

"In the morning, if at all possible, we're to move down the mountain and return to Rescue Center."

"Boss, can we do this? I mean in some spots the snow must be four feet deep already."

"Weather is calling for a break in the winds for, oh, maybe twenty-four hours or so. Then right after that, another front is moving in behind it. This next storm will be harder and last longer, according to the weather gurus. I told Center we'd make an attempt to leave in the morning."

"If we don't get out now, what you mean is, we'll be here all winter." Ben said.

"That's about the size of it. We've all seen winters here when these mountains get snowdrifts well over ten feet high. If we don't get out in this twenty-four hour window, well, have your mail forwarded to this mountain for the winter."

"When do we start?" P.W. asked.

"Right at daylight, son, and it's going to be a walk right out of hell. Ben, any suggestions about Lewis and moving?"

"No, not really, except he'll be in some pain. I have some codeine based drugs with me, enough for a week, so he'll be out of it most of the time. He'll not be able to walk unassisted, if that's what you mean."

"So, how do we move him? I know we'll have to walk and lead the horses. I'll not risk the life of a single horse on this trip."

"I see three options and none are really very good. We can tie him over a horse, we can rig a travois, or one of us can lead him as he walks. I may be able to give him a low dosage of the medication and he'll be able to walk. Lewis is a strong man, so he'll try to walk if he's given a choice."

"From one to ten, with ten being the highest, what do you think his pain level will be?"

"Each person is different, but I'd suspect about a four, or maybe up to a six. If he bumps a stub you're looking at a twelve, because he'll lose his mind."

"Okay, I don't want him on a horse, because if an animal falls off this mountain, I'll lose my son. He'll have to walk. I want you to give him the minimum of the drug, let me and Oliver lead him and we'll see how that works. Once at a lower elevation we'll tie his butt to a horse, but not up this high."

"Okay, we'll try it your way then. Now, we'll have to rotate in the lead position, because busting snow is a hard job. It's harder than it looks and I suggest we change about every twenty minutes. Once we're down lower, there will be less snow and we'll move faster."

"Sounds like a plan to me. You know, the day I promoted you to ramrod of this outfit I made the best decision in my life." Silas said.

Ben laughed and said, "I once had to walk down from a mountain after shooting a goat. I didn't want the meat to go to waste, didn't care about the horns, so I made a sled, but it didn't work very well. I did get off the mountain and brought the meat with me, but it was one tough job. I was all of maybe twenty at the time and in prime physical condition, but busting that snow liked to killed me."

"I've done it before too, and we'll have to watch for overheating. If we start to sweat, then stop; the sweat will freeze next to our skin. Hypothermia is just around the corner then."

\*\*\*\*\*

Morning dawned lung hurting cold, but with no winds and the snow had stopped. Silas and his small group were up two hours prior to sunup, packing to move. All the gear was packed on the horses and Lewis was feeling little pain due to the small white pill he'd washed down with hot coffee. Each of them had eaten two of the MRE's, because there would be no more eating until they reached safety.

As they tied gear on the horses, Silas asked, "Why couldn't you use those pills yesterday when you removed the fingers?"

"Mainly because they aren't made for the deep pain Lewis experienced yesterday. Removing a finger is painful and the best I had was a local. These pills will deaden his pain a great deal and help him move, but as I explained yesterday, since he's not used to the medication, you'll need to keep a short leash on him. If you don't, he may fall and beat us all to the bottom of this mountain."

"Like he's drunk, huh?"

"Close, but not exactly the same. It bothers all people differently, so we'll have to wait and see."

"We're all packed, boss, as soon as you two tie that to the horse." P.W. said and then smiled.

*That's likely the last smile he'll give for a day or two,* Ben thought.

Silas finished his knot and said, "I want Ed breaking snow first, then we'll rotate every twenty minutes. Take your time, we're not in a race, and for God's sake, don't slip and fall. Now, let me call Rescue Center and let them know we're moving."

His call soon finished, Silas said, "No change, so we've twenty-four hours to get off this mountain. Ed, head 'em out."

Ed started walking and did well for about five minutes, then he was heard breathing hard.

"You doin' okay?" Silas asked.

"I'm fine, uh, but this is harder than it looks."

"Take your time and when you get tired, let me know and the next person will rotate into your position."

Ed waved a glove hand and started moving again.

The morning passed slowly, with very little straight distance covered, because the mountain trail was a winding one and went up and down like a roller-coaster. Finally, near noon, Silas called for a short break. Most of them were winded and needed a rest.

"How far do you think we've come?" P.W. asked.

"Well, son, that large barren spot off our left is Piney Lake, so we're about halfway to the bottom. If all goes well, we'll soon be able to ride. Nonetheless, I won't mount a horse until we get on some level terrain."

"I can understand that, but I'm about worn out."

"What? You mean to sit there and tell me a young whippersnapper like you is bushed already?"

Lowering his head, P.W. said, "I'm tired and never thought it'd be this rough. I don't think I'm made to be in rescue and recovery."

"So, when things get rough, you want to quit on me, huh?" Silas laughed and then added, "You can't quit, not until we reach the Rescue Center anyway, and then our mission will be over. You can do this, son, because you've already completed half of it. I've been in rescue for thirty years and this is as rough as I've ever seen it get. Usually we fly in with a chopper, locate the survivors or bodies and then fly out."

"Well, on second thought, I'll stick it out until the end."

"Spoken like a real member of my team, and P.W.?"

"Yes, sir?" the young man met the older man's eyes.

"Never, and I mean *never*, quit anything you start. See, once a man starts quitting, it gets easier as he grows older. I'm over three times your age and trust me, this is rougher on my old body than it is on yours, but I never start something I won't finish. I want you to think about what I just said, and tell me later, after we return, what you think."

"Yes, sir, I'll do that."

Standing, Silas said, "Let's move out and I want Oliver leading."

It was near mid-afternoon when Ed gave a scream and started sliding down the side of the mountain. His feet kicked and his arms grabbed at everything, but he was sliding on top of the snow. Finally, he grabbed a bush as he slid by and came to a complete stop. He looked up at the group and his eyes were huge in fear.

"Ed, if I lower a rope, can you get it around you?" Silas asked.

"Not one-handed, I don't think."

"Okay, then one of use will come down for you."

"I'm scared to let go of this bush and can't do the job alone."

Oliver said, "Next to P.W., I'm the lightest so lower me down to him."

"Okay," Silas said then added, "but take your time, and you'll have two ropes. One rope will be tied around your waist and the other will be to tie around him. Tie him around the waist and then yell when you're ready. Both ropes will be tied to a saddle horn, so you won't fall far, even if you slip."

Oliver took the offered rope from P.W. and tied it around her waist. She handed the coil to her father and then said, "Keep the horses as is or you'll be short a daughter and cook this afternoon."

Silas, fighting his own fears replied, "Do like we practiced and all will go well. I love you sweetheart, but Ed needs saving."

"I know. Okay, let's get this show on the road." Oliver said and moved to the edge of the trail. Leaning back, she felt the rope grow tight, and knew her father had her in his hands. *How many times has this man held me,* she thought and felt her fears disappear.

It was slow moving to Ed, and during the last few feet, she slipped and landed right beside the man. *Oh, thank you, sweet Jesus,* she thought, as she realized her father was still holding on to her.

Glancing down, she knew snow covered the boulders below.

Looking into Ed's frightened eyes she said, "I'm going to slip this rope around your waist, so arch your back a little, if you can, and let's get you back on the trail."

"Go easy with me, Oliver; if this bush pulls loose, I'm a dead duck. It's ready to pop out any second now."

"Dad, I'm going to have Ed grab my rope, but keep the horse from moving. His bush is about ready to pull loose."

"Go ahead, you're secured."

"Now, grab my rope and I'll tie the other one around you once you've a good grip, okay?"

"I . . . I guess. Lawdy, I don't like doin' this." he said and then closed his eyes.

"Open your eyes, Ed! Doggone you, look at me! Grab this rope and do 'er now!"

Ed's eyes shot open, he reached for the rope with his left hand, got a good grip and then grabbed it with his right.

Oliver worked fast, because she knew he was terrified and she didn't blame him. One mistake and he'd fall hundreds of feet to a rough death on the snow-covered rocks below. She tied his rope securely and after the first knot was tied, she gave a prayer of thanks.

"Okay, Ed let go and relax." Oliver said, then called to her father, "Pull us up, dad, but slowly."

Silas smiled, secretly proud of his daughter and looking at Ben, he said, "Move the horse, but do the job slowly. If anything happens now, we'll lose both of them."

When she neared the edge, she helped her father raise Ed first, then up she went. Shaken up, but not overly so, she smiled and said, "Now that wasn't so bad, huh, Ed?"

He looked at her like she was crazy and said, "I'd not like to do 'er again, if ya want the truth. I ain't never been so scared in my life."

"Look, you're both alive, but let this be a lesson to all of us. All it takes is one second of not paying attention, stepping on a slick spot, or not noticing a slope and it's all over but the dying. This could have very well ended differently. Now, let's move."

# CHAPTER 12

AT the four wheelers, George was arguing with John over the radio. "I don't think it's safe for us to move."

"I know it's not safe, but it's now or never. We've got one chopper on loan from the United States Air Force and it's inbound for the survivors. They won't have room on board for all of you and your gear. As a matter of fact, I'm not even sure what model of helicopter they're sending. I heard a Huey, but don't really know. Look, leave the ATVs if you have to and walk out. But, if you think you can drive out, then do it. I don't like leaving a half-dozen ATVs all winter either, but this window is your last chance, according to the weather guys, so get out."

"I think we can drive out, but I'll have to rig something on the biggest and most powerful ATV to push the snow out of the way. If I can jury-rig a plow we'll drive out, but I'm tellin' you right now, it may be the snow is just too deep."

"Give it your best shot, okay?"

"Roger, copy and out."

George ran his fingers through his hair, put his cowboy hat back on and said, "Bob, let's get your ATV and see if we can rig up a plow, so we can drive home. We've been ordered to return to Rescue Center."

Everyone screamed with joy for a few minutes, then Bob said, "I can make a rough looking plow using hard woods by lashing them together. It won't be super strong and we may have to repair constantly on the way back."

"It'll beat walkin', right?"

"Oh, yeah, it will at that."

"Okay folks, until the plow is completed, Bob is in charge. Now, tell us what to do to make this happen."

\*\*\*\*\*

A little over an hour later, a crude plow blade was complete, but it looked like a toy for kids. Bob started his ATV and moved toward a drift of snow about three feet high and the plow worked, pushing the snow off to the side.

"We'll make another, just so we don't have to constantly stop to repair this one." George said and then smiled. They'd found a way, maybe, to drive out, but would it work well enough to get them to safety?

"Okay," George said a little later, "load all our gear and supplies. Once completed, let's move. I want us to move slowly and if you lose control of your ATV, jump clear if you can. Some of these trails have drops of five hundred feet or more. I don't need to tell you what will happen if you hit a patch of ice and go over the edge."

"I'll lead until my plow starts to break up or slip, then Church can take over. When we take a break, depending how close we are to being off the mountain, we'll repair both plows." Bob said as he moved to his ATV and mounted. His gear was already loaded and he was ready to ride.

\*\*\*\*\*

About half way down the mountain, there was a loud cracking sound and then Bob began cursing. He stopped his ATV, turned the engine off and dismounted. Moving to George he said, "I must have struck a big rock or something, because the plow just busted up on me."

Churchwell, who heard the conversation said, "Just let me take over and you follow. Later, if need be, we'll make another plow blade for your ATV."

"He's got a valid point, because I can see no reason his vehicle can't plow the snow the rest of the way; after all, you brought us this far with no problems." George said.

They continued down the treacherous mountain trail until Bob gave a loud scream and rolled from his ATV, just before it slid off the side of the mountain. Everyone stopped, Bob stood, and they could hear the vehicle bouncing off of rocks and trees below. Suddenly, there came a loud explosion and a huge fireball, rolling inside of itself, raised beside the mountain. Black oily flames rolled from the canyon to the sky.

Bob stood on the trail shaking, either from his close brush with death or the cold. No one asked, because they were shocked almost as badly. If he'd not jumped from his ATV when he did, he'd be dead right now.

George quickly called in the mishap and then, while still on the radio, said, "Roger that, base, but I wanted you to know, just in case the fire was spotted and reported to you. No, we're all safe. Do you copy?"

At Rescue Center, Barbara replied, "Understand, Wheels One, that all are okay. Will you continue to move?"

"Uh, roger that, Base, we will move. Our ETA, Echo, Tango, Alpha to your location is three hours. Copy?"

"Roger, your ETA is three hotels, over."

"Any info we need to know?"

"Roger that, John will make an attempt with the helicopter crew to get to Heather and Mike this morning, at some point. We have a Huey from the Air Force and only one. The winds are still too high in some areas of the mountains, but they should die within an hour or two."

"Copy, Base, and we're continuing to move, over."

"Base to Wheels One, you're coming in broken."

"Understand you have me broken. Must be the atmosphere. This is Wheels One, out."

"Rog— that —eels one. Go— luck. Out."

"What's wrong with the radio?" Ben asked.

"Atmospheric conditions would be my guess. It's still overcast and there are all sorts of things

in the air that can affect a radio." George relied.

"What about me, since I lost my ride?"

"Climb behind me and hang on. Now, if I leave this thing, you'd better be right behind me, okay?"

Bob laughed and when sober, he said, "You may start moving before me, but I'll hit the ground before you. I almost filled my pants when my machine headed for the edge." He shuddered after he spoke, remembering the near miss.

George called out, "Let's move, folks, we're wasting daylight."

Two hours before dusk they reached the bottom of the mountain and discovered the ground covered with about six inches of snow. Knowing they were safer now, George opened his throttle more and moved toward Rescue Center.

*****

At the Center, John was waiting impatiently for a rescue chopper. The aircraft had developed unexpected mechanical problems and was grounded until the bird could be fixed. He stood near the coffee pot and every few minutes he'd walk in a circle, as if his moving would make things happen sooner.

"Boss," Barbara said, "can you stop the pacing? You're driving me about half nuts."

John gave a light chuckle and replied, "I'm impatient and want to get those two off the mountain."

The phone rang, Barbara picked it up and said, "Hello, Rescue Center, Barbara Adams speaking."

A minute passed, with her mainly listening and then she said, "Goodbye." Turning to John and smiling, she said, "That was weather and the front is stationary right now, so it looks like we'll have another day of fine weather tomorrow, with very light winds."

"Ya-hoo!" John screamed, looked at Peter and Wendy, and then added, "We'll get them tomorrow."

Sandy met John's eyes and asked, "Will they be brought here or taken to a hospital?"

"I can't say for sure, but I want both of them taken to the closest hospital. Both sustained injuries and we have no idea how badly Heather injured her head."

"Actually, we've had no contact with either of them since Heather called her doctor." Peter said, blinked rapidly a few times, and then added, "For all we know, they could be dead, or at least one of them."

"That's always a possibility, but it's not likely. Of the two, the medical folks think Heather was in the most danger of dying. Head injuries are dangerous and while snakebite can kill, it usually only happens with the very young or old. I know Mike suffered a great deal of pain, except I'm sure he's still very much alive, because he was in excellent health. The day I dropped the supplies to them, I saw smoke from a campfire, Peter, and that tells me someone was alive on the ground."

"I'm sorry if I seemed negative, but it's been over a week. We thought this would be over in a few hours."

"Listen, most rescues are said and done within 48 hours, but in this one, well, we had bad weather, which is abnormal for this time of the year, but it does happen from time to time."

Wendy said, "John, we want to thank you and all the men and women who've given their time to search for Mike."

"We are in the rescue business, Wendy, and we'll respond any time and any place. I'm just sorry I had to meet you and Peter under these conditions."

"Do you have any idea which hospital Heather will be taken to when they do bring her out?" Sandy asked.

"No, as I said before, and I can understand your apprehension, but once they're picked up, I'll make sure the pilot radios the Center here and passes the name of the hospital on to you and the Nash family. I promise."

"Good, because I'm worried about my baby."

"I understand, and would be too, if our roles were reversed."

Barbara suddenly said, "The Air Force says their maintenance men will not be able to fix the broken bird until sometimes late tonight."

"Okay, so I suggest we all relax, get something to eat, and wait. There is absolutely nothing we can do until morning." John said and moved toward his office.

Officer Michaels stuck his head in the door and said, "Peter and Wendy, you have some members of your family here and they'd like to speak with both of you."

Both walked to the door and outside was a small group of family and friends. It was still cold out, so Wendy said, "Let us get our jackets and we'll be right out. We're so happy to see all of you."

Minutes later, as they all stood together, Wendy asked, "What is it all of you want to speak about?"

Uncle Thomas said, "We've all brought some foods so Mike can eat when they bring him out tonight." Thomas was wearing a big smile.

"They're not going for him until in the morning."

"But," Cousin Janet said, "the news on TV said —"

"Well, the news is wrong. John, the master mind behind this rescue, said the Air Force aircraft has problems and they'll not be here until in the morning."

All the smiles disappeared and then Thomas said, "Shall we pray?"

"Yes." Peter said as he hugged Wendy.

"Please, and will you lead us, Uncle Thomas?"

\*\*\*\*\*

High on the mountain, Mike and Heather sat close to the fire. Heather shook her head and said, "I have no idea why they didn't come for us today. The winds were light and they know exactly where we are too."

"Maybe the helicopter is broken."

"It could be, but that doesn't happen often."

"But, it could have happened, right?"

Giving a loud sigh, Heather replied, "Of course it could have happened."

"Don't worry, they'll come for us tomorrow. We have food and the tent, so we'll be okay until they get here."

Heather reached over and tossed Mike's hair.

*He's braver than I am,* she thought.

"What?" he asked with the trace of a smile on his face.

"You cheered me up, is what you did. I was sitting here feeling pretty low, but we've got plenty of supplies to last a lot longer. I'm just tired of my head hurting and waiting to be picked up."

"I know the feeling, but my dad always tells me that things happen when the time is right and not before. We've both prayed and asked God to send a rescue chopper for us, so they'll come."

"You're positive?"

"Sure and no doubt in my mind. God hears everyone."

"It's getting late, so eat your cookie and have a hot drink. We need to get to sleep in a few minutes, if we can. I suspect and hope if the weather is like today in the morning, they'll come for us."

"Heather?"

"What?"

"Thank you for helping me. I know you're an angel sent by God."

Heather laughed and replied, "I'm no angel, because I'm not a good enough person to be an angel."

"I think you're just fine and I know now all angels don't live in heaven with God."

Heather, feeling uncomfortable with all the talk about angels said, "Finish your cookie and let's get some sleep."

Later, after Mike had gone to his sleeping bag in the tent, she gave much thought to his words. *I've done some things in the past I'm not proud of, so why did God pick me to be with Mike? she thought. What is He wanting me to learn from this? I know there is a message. I've learned patience and the fact that one person can make a big difference in the life of another. I think, once off this mountainside, I need to speak with Minister Thomas. Perhaps he can shed some light into why I was chosen to be here. I could have just as easily been killed by the landslide that night.*

Heather sat by the fire for hours, but then stood on aching legs and made her way toward her sleeping bag, hoping tomorrow they'd finally go home.

\*\*\*\*\*

Morning dawned very cold, but with no winds that could be felt. Heather knew that up higher crosswinds might be there and that would be the deciding factor in any rescue attempt. Their camp was nested between two ridge lines, one west and the other east. It was very likely any rescue chopper would come from one of those two directions.

"How's your arm?" she asked as she neared the always hungry fire with a load of wood.

"Aches a little, but the deep pain is gone."

"Did you sleep well?"

Mike laughed and said, "Yep, but I dreamed of food. MRE's are good, but after a while they get old."

"Yep, they do, but they're keeping us alive."

"I dreamed of banana cream pie, a root beer, and steak."

"My, you must be hungry then."

"I always ate good food at home and never noticed, not really, how much I had to eat. My mom always made sure we had good meals, but I think she'd have a fit if she saw us eating with our dirty hands and faces like we do now." He pulled an MRE from the box that held them.

"We have to do it, because we can't bathe every day, not outside, and for sure not in this temperature."

"Oh, I know that, but she's strict on clean hands and faces at the supper table."

"Good, because good hygiene will help keep you healthy."

"That's what she says too. Do you really think they'll come today?" Mike asked as he opened the MRE for breakfast.

"Yes, I do and to make things easier, I'm going down the slope and see if a radio is in the bag we didn't collect."

"That's not a slope, that's a steep cliff and if you fall, you're dead."

"I have some rope and I'll tie it to my waist. I've been trained in mountain climbing and I think I can do the job safely."

"I hope they trained you to climb mountains in deep snow."

She gave a light laugh and said, "Nope, it didn't cover snow, but if I can reach a radio, maybe we can find out what is planned for the day and help when they come for us."

"Heather?"

"Huh?"

"Please be safe, okay? If it gets too dangerous, don't take any chances. I couldn't live knowing your death was because I got lost. Will you promise me?"

"Yes, I promise if it looks dangerous I'll climb back up, okay?"

"Good. I feel better already."

"Eat, and then we'll get the radio."

Mike finished his meal in no time, because they were both always hungry.

Seeing him finish, Heather said, "I've got the rope, so let's go."

Once at the gorge, she noticed it seemed steeper and deeper than before. She suspected it was just a little over seventy-five feet to the bottom, and her rope was a hundred, so it'd work. When she glanced at Mike, he looked scared.

"I'm going to tie one end of the rope to a big tree and lower myself to the bottom. Once at the bag, I'll go through it and see if it contains anything we need. If so, I'll put the small stuff in my pockets and the big things in the bag. I'll then climb back up and pull the bag up."

Mike nodded, not liking the idea at all. The sides of the cliff were covered in ice and snow and he knew just one slip and he'd be alone again, with Heather either seriously hurt or dead.

Heather moved to a large pine, tied the rope around it and then moved to the edge.

"Heather, before you start down, I want you to know I've prayed for you."

She smiled and said, "I've prayed too." She then jumped backwards from the edge, and was instantly lost to sight.

Mike moved as close to the edge as he dared, looked down and saw her descending in a controlled fashion. A couple of minutes later, she stood beside the bag. He watched as she squatted and unzipped the canvas container. He couldn't tell what she was removing, because it was all packed in plastic and vacuum sealed.

He watched as she placed things in her coat and cargo pockets of her military style pants.

Minutes later, she yelled, "I'm coming back up!"

She grabbed the rope and began to ascend, which made Mike nervous. About half way to the top, her right foot slipped, she fell to the left and impacted the edge, hard. Ice and snow fell and crashed on the rocks below. She swung from side to side for a few minutes and then started back up. When she reached the top, Mike saw blood running from the left sleeve of her coat.

"A . . . are you okay?" he asked.

"I think I knocked some skin off of my left elbow, but I'm fine."

"Hurting?"

"A little, but nothing is broken." she replied.

"What did you find?"

"Some odds and ends. I found a bag of chocolate bars, some hot coco, and a radio. There are two spare batteries too."

"Are you going to try it now?" Mike asked with a big smile.

"No, let's get back to camp and then we'll give it a try. First, I have to clean and bandage my arm."

Back at camp, Heather moved close to the fire, removed her coat and rolled her shirt sleeve up. There was a long scrape near the elbow, so she heated some water to clean it. As the water warmed up, she pulled out some triple antibiotic ointment and gauze from the first aid supplies. When the water was warm to her touch, she pulled the pot from the fire and said, "Use this clean rag and wash my injury. I don't see any debris in the wound so more or less run water over it to irrigate it a little."

Ten minutes later, her arm dried, wrapped, and back in her coat, she pulled out the radio and said, "Shall we give this thing a try?"

# CHAPTER 13

"JOHN, come quick! I have Heather on the radio!" Barbara said with a big smile. She'd been reading a paperback novel when the radio suddenly came alive.

John moved to the radio and Barbara place the receiver on speaker.

"Rescue Center, this is Heather Edwards, do you read, over?"

John said, "Heather, this is Rescue Center One, good to hear from you. What is your condition, over?"

Barbara gave a little happy dance in her chair and gave John a thumb up.

"We're both okay, that's Oscar, uh, hotel. I mean Oscar, uh, oh, kilo, Oscar Kilo. Mike is fine and with me."

"Understand you are both in good condition, correct?"

"Uh, some minor injuries, but nothing life threatening. So, that's a big Roger on our conditions."

"We will make a rescue attempt at some point today. The Air Force will be sending a Huey and it's likely they'll use a forest penetrator, copy?"

"Copy. What is your ETA?"

"Not sure. The aircraft is still undergoing maintenance. I'll radio you before we depart this station."

"Roger that and copy. I'll monitor for contact fifteen minutes before and after each hour until dusk."

"Understand. Do you have any pressing needs at this time? I repeat, any needs at this time?"

"No, uh, negative, all is well."

"This is Rescue Center One, out."

"Out." Heather said.

Turing to Joshua Boozer, the Pararescueman, John said, "Find the Nash family and Sandy Edwards. Have them meet me here."

"Uh, Sandy is in the living room watching television, so all you need is the Nash family. The last time I saw them, they were praying with some other family members outside."

"Fetch 'em, Josh."

Ten minutes later, with all three of them in the living room of the mobile camper, John said, "I just spoke with Heather on the radio."

All smiled and Peter lowered his head and said, "Praise God."

"Now," John said, "they're both in good condition with only some minor injuries. Neither, according to Heather are in bad shape."

"John!" Barbara yelled, "the Air Force has a rescue bird inbound. ETA is twenty mike. Aircraft is a Huey, tail number niner, niner, six, seven, niner, with a P.J. on board and a forest penetrator."

"Great! Barbara, contact weather and get the latest information they may have. Let me know the status immediately."

"Sure."

"This is happening so fast now. What does all of this mean?" Wendy asked, her fears coming alive again.

"It means, God willing, we'll have a shot at getting your boy and Heather out of the mountains today at some point. Let's hope the winds remain calm and if so, you'll be having supper with him this evening. Remember, they're both fine, according to Heather and she's been trained in basic first aid, so she'd know."

"Boss! Weather says what we have now will continue up until after midnight. Still cold, 12 degrees, but with a very light wind. They have no crosswinds noted for the mountain passes right now, but as you know, that could change quickly."

"Mr and Mrs Nash, and Mrs Edwards, I have to dress for the rescue. So please excuse me."

As John walked to his office, he heard Wendy sobbing with happiness and Sandy talking with

Peter. *I hope,* he thought, *we don't let these people down. In all my years, this has been the longest non-combat rescue attempt I've ever worked.*

Turning, John said, "Barbara, try to contact Heather at fifteen minutes before the hour and let her know we're coming to bring them out. Remind her we want the Nash boy first, then her, because he's the youngest. Change her call sign from Heather to Survivor One."

\*\*\*\*\*

At fifteen before the hour, Heather turned the radio on and immediately heard Barbara's voice, "Heather, this is Rescue Center, over."

"Go center, this is Heather."

"Good to hear from you again. Your call sign is now Survivor One, copy?"

"Copy, and I'm Survivor One."

"Ask them when they're coming for us, please." Mike asked as he stood next to her.

"They'll tell us when to get ready." she replied and then added, "Now be quiet, so I can hear the radio."

"Survivor One, you are to prepare for pickup. Do you copy?"

Smiling, Heather said, "Roger that! ETA?"

"Unknown at this time, but send Mike up first on the penetrator, copy?"

"Copy, Rescue Center, and Mike is the first passenger to ride up."

"Roger, and stay tuned to this frequency for direct contact from the chopper."

"Understand and will maintain radio discipline and stay on this frequency."

"I can hear the Air Force chopper nearing now, so they'll not be long. Survivor One, both you and Survivor Two, will be taken to the nearest hospital first, copy?"

"Copy, Rescue Center, and may God bless you!"

"Any questions?"

"No, uh, negative."

"Okay, Survivor One, your next radio contact should be with the chopper."

"Good to hear, Center."

"This is Rescue Center, out."

Turning to Mike, Heather gave a big smile and said, "They're coming for us. Now, we need to pick up debris or things laying around that may be blown by the rotor blades. Can you help me? Oh, and you'll go up first."

"What do you mean, go up?" he asked as they started picking up clothing, empty MRE wrappers and other trash they had around camp.

154

"They'll have a forest penetrator that'll come down from the chopper when it hovers above us. Let it touch the ground before you touch it, or the static electricity will knock you for a loop. You, and I'll help you, need to lower a seat, pull out a strap and place it under your arms and around you. Then they'll raise you to the door of the aircraft. You do nothing, but sit. They'll then pull you into the chopper and lower the device to me."

"Sounds easy."

"If you're scared of heights, just close your eyes. I've done it many times and its fun, actually."

"It doesn't sound hard."

"It's not hard, but do exactly what they tell you or you could fall from the aircraft."

"I'd guess so. No, I want to get home safely, so I'll listen."

"Good and we're going to a hospital first, I guess to be checked out by a team of doctors."

"I don't like that at all." Mike said.

"Look, it's the only way they can make sure we're able to go home and you *do* want to go home don't you?"

Lowering his head, Mike said, "Yup, I do. I'll do it, but I won't like it."

"I'll be the one getting shots, because of my injuries and I might even have to stay in the hospital."

"If you are, I'll come and see you every day. I promise, because yo—"

"Hush, do you hear that?"

Silence.

Finally, Mike said, "It sounds like a motor."

"I'm not sure, but I think that's our ride home."

"Survivor One, this is Save One, over."

Picking the radio up, she said, "Save One, I've been expecting you."

"My ETA to your last know position is in approximately five mikes. I'll do a flyover to mark your position; do you know how to do that?"

"Roger that."

"Since neither of you are seriously injured, we'll use a penetrator to lift you up, or do you need assistance?"

Smiling, Heather said, "Negative on assistance. Are we still to come up one at a time?"

"Negative, I say again, negative. Both of you mount the seats at the same time. Do you copy?"

"Copy loud and clear, Save One."

The pilot kept her talking, mainly to keep her spirits up and finally said, "I'm starting my approach to your last known positions, so give me a countdown, over."

"Five, four, three, two, uh, one, you are overhead . . . now!"

"Good job, Survivor One, we have you visual and marked on our map. On my next approach, we'll pick you up. I want to thank you for flying Tree Top Airlines today."

Heather and Mike both laughed and the young man began to jump up and down with joy.

A few minutes later, the chopper stopped directly over them and a long thin object was lowered. The engines of the aircraft made communication hard for the two on the ground, so when Mike moved for the penetrator, she yelled, "Let it hit the ground first. Remember the static electricity."

He nodded and waited.

As soon as the device struck the ground, Heather moved to it, unzipped some things and pulled out straps. She'd already lowered what looked like paddles and motioned for Mike to join her.

"Sit on a paddle and let me route this strap around you. No matter what happens, hang on and don't do anything they don't tell you to do."

He nodded.

She then positioned herself on a seat, ran the strap around her, and gave a thumbs up. Almost immediately, they started to rise. Mike closed his eyes and waited. After about a minute, someone grabbed them and pulled them inside the chopper. Hands were all over them as they unhooked the straps, folded the chairs, and moved both survivors to red canvas seats along a wall of the aircraft. A man wearing a helmet, with a clear visor down, moved to them and strapped them in.

Finally, the man in the helmet said, "P.J. to aircraft commander, we have secured the survivors."

"Roger that, Steve, so I'll head for General Hospital and deliver our passengers."

The trip passed quickly, maybe too quickly, for Mike who was busy watching the pilot and other men do their jobs. One man, like the rest, wore a green jumpsuit, and was sitting opposite them in the chopper. Mike recognized him as the man who'd pulled him inside the aircraft. When the man caught Mike looking at him, he flashed a thumb up. Mike returned the sign.

Finally, a man neared and held up 5 fingers. He said something, but the noise inside the aircraft was incredible. Mike took it to mean they'd land in five minutes.

Heather leaned over and yelled in his ear, "We land in five minutes. We're going to the hospital first."

Mike nodded.

*****

The chopper came to a stop in the air, slowly lowered to the tarmac with a light bump, and a few minutes later, the loud whine of the engines grew silent. The pilot turned his head, and smiled as he said, "Welcome home. There is an ambulance outside that will take both of you to the hospital, where you'll be given a thorough looking over."

The man with the clear visor in the back said, "Now the engines are quiet, I'm Sergeant Jonas Culvert and I'm the P.J. for this flight. If you'll both come with me, we'll meet the ambulance."

The side door opened and the three of them entered the rear of the vehicle. Mike had seen a group of reporters with cameras behind a roped off area, so he asked, "Who are all those people?"

Jonas replied, "Reporters from all over the world. You two are famous and I suspect you'll not get a minute of peace once you leave the base."

The ride to the hospital was short, just a few minutes, and when they arrived, other reporters were there too, but roped off again. Two medical technicians arrived with wheelchairs and both were told to sit, it was a hospital requirement. They were immediately wheeled into separate rooms and each had a medical staff and a doctor.

Mike's condition was listed as good because he was a bit dehydrated and his electrolytes were low, so an IV was started. Overall, he was in good condition and when the doctor asked him if he needed anything, the young man asked, "Can I have a steak?"

"Hungry, are you?"

"Yes, sir. We had MRE's, but I've wanted a steak for days."

Smiling the doctor turned to a nurse and said, "Sara, see this young man gets the thickest steak we have and I see no reason to limit his solid food intake. They've both been eating solids, so this won't hurt him and may even cheer him up a little."

"I'll see he gets one." Sara said and then left.

"Your snakebite is almost completely healed. Is it causing you any problems?" the doctor asked.

"No, not really, but it scared me when I started swelling. I thought my arm was going to explode."

"Pain was rough too, huh?"

"Yep, but that's all gone now."

"Well, Mr. Nash, as soon as you eat your steak and your IV is done, you can go home."

"What about my friend, Heather?"

"Honestly, I don't know, but I will find out for you. She may have to stay a few days, because head injuries can be very serious and tests will have to be done. Let me see what her doctor has to say and I'll let you know."

When the doctor left, so did everyone else.

A few minutes later the doctor returned and said, "Your friend will be staying with us a few days. Overall she is okay, but as I said before, we need to run some tests and make sure she'll be okay."

"A few times in the woods she screamed, fell to the ground, and then had a fit. I was scared she'd die or not wake up."

"She suffered a serious injury and in most cases it should have killed her."

"She didn't die, because she's an angel."

"Do you think so?" the doctor asked with a smile.

"Yep, I do."

"Look what I have." Nurse Sara said as she entered the room and placed a meal on a small table beside his bed. Moving the table in front of Mike, she continued, "Steak, baked potato, salad, carrots, and fresh baked bread. Oh, and some milk."

The doctor wrote something in Mike's chart and left the room.

The nurse adjusted his dripping IV and then left the room. Mike discovered he was unable to eat the whole meal. The steak was huge and he was unable to eat it all. He'd just wiped his mouth off, when the door opened and in walked his mother and father. Mike lowered his head, suspecting he was in trouble.

His mother moved quickly to him, kissed his cheeks and said, "Oh, Mike, we were worried sick about you. Are you okay?"

"I'm fine, but I sure caused a big mess, huh? I know I'm grounded for years." He began to cry, not so much in fear, but with the sudden understanding he was with his parents—and safe.

"Son, what makes you think you're in trouble?" Dad asked.

"I tried to walk back to camp alone and didn't tell a scout leader I was leaving."

"We spoke to both Frank Bailey and Ira Banks and neither are mad at you. While Frank said it's against the rules in scouting to do what you did, most of the boys do it all the time. Now, once this is reported to those higher up in scouting, well, something might be said. But, I doubt it will change anything in your pack, other than all members being reminded to obey the rules in the future."

"I heard some people were hurt and killed looking for me. Is that true?"

"Yes and no, son. There was an earthquake and there were deaths as a result of a rock slide and not you." Father replied, gave a light smile and added, "Mike, it was the will of God and not your fault."

"If they hadn't been looking for me, they would still be alive."

"Son, before we're born, God knows to the second how long each of us will live. I don't know how many were killed or are just missing. With bad weather hitting right after the rock slide, it will take some time to see who eventually turns up, and who has perished."

The doctor entered, gave a big smile and said, "Mike, I have signed your discharge and you're free to leave with your mom and dad."

"When?"

"Well, as soon as I get a nurse to remove your IV you're cleared to leave. I do suggest you use the parking lot exit to avoid reporters. You're hot news, son, and all of them want to talk to you."

Mike nodded and the doctor left.

"Hungry?" Mom asked.

"No, I just had a big steak. I'd like a hot shower, clean clothes and some time relaxing. I'm suddenly very tired."

# CHAPTER 14

THE next day at home Mike's father walked into the living room and said, "John Smith, the Rescue Center Commander, has scheduled an interview with a reporter this afternoon at four. You, Heather, your mother and I will be there."

"Dad, I don't want to go."

"Mike, sooner or later you'll have to speak about your adventure. Let's get it over with and then the reporters will stop hanging around our driveway at all hours."

"I know it has to be done, but what if they ask a question I don't know anything about?"

"That is why John, your mother and I will be there. I'll not let you look bad or say something you don't mean if you get confused. It'll be fine, son. You might even enjoy it."

"Heather will be there, son." Mom said.

"I would like to see Heather again, because she saved my life."

"You called her an angel last night. So, I have something to give you." His mother handed him a small golden angel pin, with a small diamond near the halo. "This was your great-grandmother's and she was an angel too. I think it'd be nice to give this to Heather as a way of saying thank you."

"Wow, mom, is it expensive?" Mike asked as he held it in his hand.

"A little, but your life is worth much more to me. I want you to give it to her, son."

Mike smiled and then said, "Okay, I'll do it."

*****

They all arrived at Rescue Center thirty minutes early and Mike immediately noticed a podium with a microphone in front of the RV. The reporters, some of which even followed dad's truck to the briefing, were kept back by state police and ropes. John met them at the truck and escorted them into the long vehicle.

Once inside, Mike spotted Heather. When he walked to her, she stood and hugged him.

Reaching into his coat pocket, he pulled the pin out and said, "For my angel."

Heather laughed, thanked him, and then showed it to her mother. Turning back to Mike she pinned it on and said, "I'll wear it for you."

"Okay," John said, "most of the briefing will be conducted by me. Each of you, especially Mike and Heather, will be asked questions. If any of you are asked a question you don't understand or know the answer to, then refer the question to me. Simply say you should or need to ask that question to Mr. Smith."

Mike was grinning because he felt good giving the angel to Heather and with her with him, he knew he could face the reporters.

A few minutes later, Barbara said, "It's time for the press meeting, sir."

With John leading, they left the RV and made their way to the podium. Once in place, John cleared his throat and said, "Standing behind me are two survivors that we spent days attempting to rescue and finally did. Due to weather, we were on hold for most of that time and I'm very happy, indeed, to tell you that both will live. This was a costly rescue, with thousands of dollars in equipment dropped to the survivors, resources and fuel costs, and even the loss of one additional life due to a heart attack triggered by an earthquake. Our earlier report of three missing searchers has been corrected. They were all recovered over time and all of our folks have now been accounted for. Let me introduce first Mike Nash, the goal of our search efforts, and then Heather Edwards, a member of our staff who was severely injured the night of the quake, and who eventually found this brave young man. Mike."

Mike move to the microphone and stood, very nervous. Heather, sensing his awkwardness in the situation walked to his side and said, "I'm Heather Edwards."

Questions were asked and either Mike or Heather answered them and then one reporter asked, "What was the name of the man killed?"

"We've prepared a listing for all of you with the names of all injured and the two fatalities. They will be available after the briefing." John replied as he quickly stepped forward.

Finally, after almost an hour, the questions stopped, Heather took a deep breath and said, "Mike and I would like to say thank you to the Rescue Center, John Smith, and all the teams who looked for us. We'd also, more importantly, like to thank God for saving us. It's easy for people sitting in warm homes, following a hot meal and hot shower, to not think about a higher power, thinking they are the sole provider for themselves, but that thought is erroneous. Mike and I, both injured, know as sure as there are stars in the sky, that God played the key role in our rescue. My doctor said my injury could and should have killed me, but it didn't. Mike could have died from exposure, because after being bitten by the snake he was in and out of consciousness. The temperature was well below zero most nights we were on this mountain, but here we stand before you. We thank you for your time."

While the reporters looked confused, Mike walked to her side, took her hand in his, and said, "Let's go to my house, Angel, momma baked some chocolate chip cookies this morning."

*The End,*

but read on to hear the real story of Jared Ropelato.

# TRUE STORY OF JARED ROPELATO AND HIS SURVIVAL

Note: Taken from information written by Jared's mother and father, Dawn and Larry Ropelato, Jared, and others, but edited for flow. Used with permission.

## PART 1

### Dawn Ropelato's story for Friday, August 12, 2011

It was Friday, August 12, 2011, close to 1pm when I got a call from my son, Justin, who told me his dad had just received a call that had notified him our son, Jared, was lost in the mountains.

"He was fishing with the rest, but headed back to camp alone. I think he'll be fine and we'll find him." Justin said, attempting to sugar coat his statements.

"This will strengthen Jared's testimony of prayer," I replied, and while I tried not to sound scared, I was and started crying.

I was to learn later my husband and Justin almost flew to the scout camp, driving as fast as they could, or as fast as the winding and twisting road and our Excursion would allow. My husband, Larry, later said at one point they were doing 99 miles an hour and would have gone faster, but that wasn't to be.

After talking with Justin, I went to the computer and went on Facebook to request prayers for my son. I was home and felt so helpless at the time, but had faith in the Lord's hand. Soon Jared's being lost was posted all over the internet and prayers started pouring in. I was comforted by the prayers, yet worried, and knew my faith in God was being tested. I was a typical mother, in that my son was lost and my biggest nightmare was coming true. I tried to hold back the tears and fears, but how many times I cried, I honestly can't say.

It was then, I remembered the other scouts and the leaders of my son's group. I suddenly felt for them and my heart went out to each of them. I'd worry about my son, his scout leaders, the boys along on the trip, and my family. My mind was racing so fast with different thoughts clouding my thinking.

I sat in my chair and thought, *Oh, the leaders and kids must be going through hell right now, with him lost. I can remember the time, years back, when I lost a friend's child at Lagoon and how terrible I felt. I told Larry it would've been easier to lose our own child. I feel awful for the leaders.*

Then, I began to believe Jared would be okay, and that he'd be found.

Soon, the media began to call, wanting to get his story out and I agreed, because I wanted as much help as possible for my son. Then, love and prayers began to flow on the computer sites where I'd posted our situation. I'd been getting texts since I'd posted and all made me feel the need for a good hug.

Naline Lee, was soon at my door, and when I saw her, I asked, "Did you come to give me a big hug?"

She smiled and said, "Sure."

She held me tightly and hugged me, as we both cried.

Minutes later, other folks began to show up and things turned busy, which was a great distraction for me. Then, the news crews arrived and things became very confusing. I received a call that said my son had just been found, then another saying he'd not been found. I was riding an emotional roller-coaster and before too long, I realized my son would not be found before dark.

Others, those who were praying for Jared, told me they knew he'd be found safe, but didn't know when he'd be found. Honestly, I wasn't overly worried about his well-being, because I'd discovered an inner peace from God, so I was fairly calm as things happened all around me. The many prayers strengthened me and I knew if I was stronger, so was Jared, the men looking for him, and other scouts.

Then I was watching the news and there on the screen was my son, Jared. I broke into a sob, because there are always missing scouts, but this one is my son. Usually, we didn't know the missing scout, but there was his image, with his name and smile, and it tore at my heart strings.

The night was passing so quickly for me, but thank goodness for my friends who took over my phones. Keri and Sabrina Gray took care of my texts and responded to each and every one. My friends Shirley and Laverna answered the incoming calls, while Natalie kept Facebook up to date for me. There was no way I could do all the things that needed to be done, so their help was greatly appreciated.

At one point, President Malone was there keeping in touch with others and he was a great comfort to me. President Malone and Paul Widdison gave me a blessing, too, which saddened me later, because my husband needed a blessing as well. I did find out later he was given one.

After the help of all my friends, the prayers by countless others, and blessings, I realized God was in charge and very much aware of our needs. I was greatly comforted by all that was going around me. God was well aware of our situation and what happened now was up to Him.

It was after midnight before the media was gone and it was almost time for me to leave. I decided I didn't want to spend another day answering phones and didn't like waiting to hear news from others. When Shirley offered to take me to the rescue center, I agreed. I wanted to be on the spot when Jared was found, not waiting at home.

Natalie was with me; she's a real sweetheart and I appreciated her support too. I quickly showered, and then we laid on the bed and talked for awhile. Once I was close to leaving, I posted on Facebook and was surprised by how many people were still awake at 1:45 in the morning. I knew many were awaiting word on my son and I knew then, many besides me, were going to lose sleep this night.  Another friend had room for my daughter, Kimberly, and took her with them for the night.

*****

**Larry Ropelato's story for Friday, August 12, 2011**

Larry, Jared's dad, received a call around 1:15 pm that Jared was lost.

I went into the furnace room, as soon as the conversation ended and said a prayer for my son.  I then informed my son, Justin, and we left work, driving to Wyoming.  As we moved, the Daggett County Sheriff's department called and stated they'd meet us there.  When Justin called Dawn, she thought he was joking with her.

I took the phone and said, "This is true, but he'll be fine, because he camps there often.  He'll be found and once located, I'll let you know.  Remember, phone reception in the mountains is poor, so it may be a while before I can call you back with good news."

After ending the call, Justin said, "I tried to sugarcoat telling her, but it's hard to do."

"You did just fine."

We were soon driving at speeds of 80-90 MPH, and sometimes 99 MPH, but then the governor would kick in and we'd slow down.

Later, as we neared the town of Mountain View, I said, "We need to stop and get some supplies we'll need."

"What do we need?"

"Gas, food, water, and flashlights.  We'll not stop long."

Justin was in and out in a few short minutes, with all I thought we needed, and we were soon on the road again.  Further down the road we ran out of pavement and were now on a dirt road.  I thought about the money I'd used to purchase what we needed for this trip. *It's a good thing I've carried a hundred dollar bill in my wallet since we were first married, just for emergencies. Being prepared was smart.*

We traveled on the dirt road at about 60 MPH, until the car slid as we went around a bend, and I thought, *I need to slow down or we'll not get there alive.*

When we arrived and got out of the car, Scoutmaster Ronnie Widdison approached and said, "I'm sorry this happened."

"It's okay." I replied, but he kept apologizing and I suspected he blamed himself, but I didn't blame anyone.

We embraced, shed a few tears, and then he went back to saying he was sorry. I tried to comfort him and let him know I understood his feelings, but he was deeply concerned.

I glanced around, and saw President Kim Christensen and his family there. They were there camping as well and were ready to go out looking for Jared too. I also noticed a high adventure group, the Farr West Stake, camping there as well.

Ronnie approached this group, because he saw they had horses and told them as they ate that we needed help finding a lost scout. They immediately stopped eating, mounted and left to search for my son.

We then organized for the hike to the scout camp; we'd have to bring our gear, but before we left, President Christensen said the most beautiful prayer. He asked God to allow us to find Jared and that he would be found safe and sound. I was touched by the man's simple but powerful words.

It was close to four miles to the camp, perhaps a little more or less, but rough country with marshes, huge boulders the size of cars, and a difficult walk, even on the designated trail.

*If our Heavenly father listens to anyone, it will be Dawn and RaeAnn Christensen, because the two of them have such strong faith. I really think those two praying for him are the best that could happen to Jared right now,* I thought as I moved slowly up the trail.

After about two miles from the scout camp, we all split up and began looking for my son. We would yell his name and then pause to listen, but heard no reply. We all continued moving toward camp as we looked for my son.

Justin said, "I'm going to go straight through the forest to the ridge, then I'll circle the ridge on the bowl. If I get lost, don't worry about me, because I know I can find my way back."

I thought for a second and then replied, "Okay, since you know the area well."

Looking back at all that happened that day, I'm not so sure that letting Justin do that was a smart decision on my part. We could have ended up looking for two of my sons, but at the time his suggestion made sense to me.

As we neared the scout camp, I thought, *Jared may be embarrassed and hiding close to camp.* I then knelt in prayer behind a large rock, asking for His help and guidance. As I prayed, I could hear helicopters off in the distance searching for my son.

I stood, looked around and thought, *This area is so thick with growth, trees and fallen trees, that the only way they'll see Jared is if he's in a marsh.*

When I entered camp I think all of us looked scared and worried. No sooner had I walked into camp than Brent Taylor and Ken Edwards, scout leaders, walked to me and gave me a hug. Both were so worried about my son that tears were flowing down their cheeks.

"Look," I said, "I don't blame anyone for this and it's not your fault, neither of you. It's one of those things that just happens." I could feel their sorrow.

While they relaxed a little at my words, I could see they were still deeply concerned, and I could understand their feelings. Shortly after I arrived we all started moving away from camp, lined up, as we went down hill, searching. We all kept the person to our left and right in sight at all times, because the forest was so thickly grown. The last thing we needed was for another person to become lost too.

As I moved through the forest, I started getting text messages, and this was an area that I'd never been able to get reception in the past. The messages were stating, 'You are in our prayers and we love you.' So, imagine my surprise, because at that moment I was struggling and needed a little extra help.

My brother also text messaged me and said he'd cover the cost of hiring an additional helicopter to look for Jared in the morning. He went on to say he was sorry he couldn't help us search, because of his bad leg. I was touched by his text and felt blessed.

As we walked, we'd call out to Jared, and I think now, in retrospect, if we'd stopped after we called out and waited for him to reply, we would have had better results. However, we never considered the noise we were making at the time. As we moved, we were stepping on branches, kicking leaves, and making more noise than we realized. I now think our searching for Jared was like prayer. Often we call out to God in prayer, but we don't stop, wait, and listen for an answer from Him. We are always in a such a big hurry to do what needs to be done next in our lives.

Moving through the thick foliage, I began to think of the problems and trials I'd had over the last week with ward issues. While working with the ward family, I always considered what can I learn from this experience? I decided to use the same approach here, in the woods. But, just minutes later, I thought, *my family is more important than the ward family. I've been putting more into the ward family than my own eternal family.*

After about an hour, I ran into President Christensen, Justin, and Jared Simpson, the father of one of the other scouts. Simpson had been out looking on his own when we ran into him. He hugged me, said he was sorry, so I told him it wasn't anyone's fault.

Now, we'd not stopped long, but when I glanced around the others in our group had continued on. We then moved off in a different direction, having no idea where the main group had gone. Justin and I were planning on spending the night at Daggett Lake, the scout camp, but most of the others were heading down hill, to their main camps at Spirit Lake.

It was then the radio we carried came alive and we heard a voice say, "We got 'em."

We all turned around and returned to Daggett Lake as quickly as the terrain would allow.

We ran into Brent Taylor, so I asked him to text Judy, who in turn could text Dawn and let her know our son had been found.

"Are you sure you want to do this?" Brent asked.

"Yes, but why not?"

"I think we should wait until we're positive he's been found."

"I know he's been found, because I heard it myself over the radio."

"Are you really sure about this?"

I thought for a few seconds and then said, "Yes, she needs to know right now."

He nodded and sent a text message.

When we arrived at the scout camp I thought Jared would be there, but we were disappointed to find he wasn't to be seen. We then assumed the rescuers had taken him to Spirit Lake.

Brent said, "We need to gather in prayer and not be like the nine lepers who didn't thank the Lord."

I spoke the prayer and made it a prayer of gratitude, but I didn't feel the "spirit" at all—I felt nothing.

Justin and I then went to Jared's tent, gathered all his belongings, and then prepared to return to Spirit lake with his stuff. We divided his gear and clothes, so each could carry some.

During the walk down the mountain side, I wondered why I felt nothing when I'd prayed giving thanks for Jared being found. The trip was too fast and hard on me and I was sweating all over his clothing, which was a mistake because the dogs trained to track my son needed his scent, not mine. As we neared the end, my legs began to cramp from exertion and exhaustion, but I couldn't stop, because I wanted to see my son safe. I kept moving, because I had to touch and speak with my boy to confirm he was okay.

Near a quarter mile from the camp, we were contacted and informed that Jared *had not* been found and it was a mistake. I was devastated and know the others with me felt the same, by their comments and expressions. A light in my brain suddenly came on and I realized why I'd felt empty after my prayer of thanks; it was because God had not yet rescued my son.

Later in camp on Spirit Lake, I discovered the comments heard on the radio did not apply to Jared, but for a searcher that had separated from the main group. We now had less than an hour of dusk left and I knew we would look no more on this day. Shortly after this, Scott and Pat arrived with Jackets and sandwiches for Justin and I. I took a sandwich, sat down on a large rock and prepared to eat, but my whole body suddenly began to shake and shiver. I suspected, but wasn't really sure, that I was going into shock.

Pat and Sarah Wolford sat next to me and Pat put her arms around me, as Sarah held my hand. Then Mike Jones and his kids showed up. They walked to me and gave their support in finding Jared. None of us had phone reception where we were, but Mike did. I called Dawn and said, "It was a mistake and Jared has not been found, yet. Our search will continue early in the morning, at first light."

"Okay, Bishop, what inspiration have you received? What is going to happen next?"

This was a very difficult phone call for me, knowing I was hurting my wife because our son had not been found, but someone else. I replied, "All I know is that Jared will not be found tonight", and I was positive of this.

No sooner had the call ended than a news station showed up and wanted to speak with a spokesman. Since Jared was my son, I decided I'd speak to them, even if my eyes were red, I was tired, and my face drawn out. Mike and Brandon then gave me a blessing and while I do not remember a single word of what was said, I did gain my strength back.

Officially the search was terminated for the night and I was asked to bring any clothing I had of my lost son's to them so the dogs could get his scent. I knew the clothing I'd carried was soaked with my sweat and useless to the dogs, but going through his pack I found a pair of dirty work socks. I placed them in a plastic baggie to seal his odor in the cotton material.

\*\*\*\*\*\*

**Jared Ropelato's story for Friday, August 12, 2011**

I was fishing at Daggett Lake and a fish broke my line, taking my lure. I asked others around me, including the leaders of our group, if they had a lure I could use. No one did, because they were fly fishing, while I was not.

"I have more lures in camp, if I can go get some." I said, hoping I could return to get it and catch a fish. I knew camp was close and it wasn't very far.

"Sure, go get your lures." one of the leaders replied and then all the leaders went over the directions to camp with me. There were just two paths so it sounded simple to me, but I then made a serious mistake. I looked for my buddy, since we always used the buddy system, and didn't see him, so I went alone.

*I hope I don't get into trouble for not bringing my buddy. Trenton Moyes, my usual buddy, remained in camp and didn't come with me, but I had another buddy while fishing.*

*I'll not be gone long anyway, so I will be fine,* he thought as he moved toward camp.

Over ten minutes passed when one of the leaders, Jared Simpson, said, "He should be back by now, so I'll go check on him."

Simpson left and returned a short time later to say, "He didn't make it to camp."

Another adult leader, Brent Taylor asked, "Is anyone at camp right now?"

"Three other boys and Ken Edwards is there too. He has been for over forty-five minutes. No one has seen Jared, so he must have taken the wrong trail." Simpson said and had a very concerned look on his face.

Brent Taylor knew time was of essence, since it was 11:30 am, so he called out to the Scoutmaster, "Ronnie, we have a problem. We have a missing boy and we need to start looking for him."

Ronnie Widdison, the Scoutmaster, was fishing about fifty yards away and asked, "Who is missing?"

"Jared Ropelato!"

"We need to start looking for him, and *now!*" Ronnie replied.

I knew I was lost, but like a lot of lost people, I kept moving, because I was scared and knew I was in trouble. I wanted to find my own way out, so I continued to move.

Children and elderly may know they need to stop where they are when lost and wait for rescue, but often they keep moving hoping to walk to safety; rarely does this happen. Jared's continuing to move is very typical for a lost child.

As I meandered on the trail, I constantly prayed for help, and the seriousness of my situation began to sink into my mind. At one point I heard someone yelling my name and I cried out a reply, but they didn't hear me. This writer suspects the searchers kept moving, not waiting quietly and listening for a reply, so the noise as they walked masked Jared's reply.

I was given hope, because I knew then they were looking for me now. I have no idea what time I heard them calling my name, but it wasn't late yet. Later, the same day I heard helicopters flying overhead, but the trees were so thick above me I only saw one, and it was red and white.

As I walked and tried to find my way back to camp, the leaders of our group got the other campers near us involved in looking for me. Soon everyone in the area was searching.

I'd been told in scouts by one of the leaders that if I got lost to follow a stream or river, because they all lead to a lake. Well they don't, because the one I followed led to a small pond. I continued to follow the small stream from the pond, as it twisted and turned running down the mountain. It was difficult to follow the stream, because the terrain was rough and marshy at times.

At one point, I went up the mountain a ways to see if I could spot my camp. I knew camp was located in a clump of trees. *This is not good,* I thought as I saw about seven clumps of thick trees, *so which is mine? Which is the right one?*

I continued to follow the stream, which I learned later was the proper thing to do, because that was exactly what the search and rescue folks thought I'd do. I learned later that by following the water down the mountain, I did exactly as predicted and came out where they were hoping I would. I guess by taking the wrong path, I really didn't, because my wrong path was the correct one in the end.

Then it began to grow dark and I became concerned, because I had very little gear with me.

# PART 2

**Jared's story continues.**

As darkness neared, I knew I had a rough and cold night coming. I knew my scout leaders and other scouts would be worried, along with my parents, but they'd be praying for me too. I started trying to remember all I could about staying alive and survival. I'd been taught a lot, but now I struggled to remember every single word.

I constructed a lean-to out of brush, dead branches, and sticks. While it was ugly, I knew it would work. I then dug a hole in the ground in the shape of my body and at times, I'd get in it to check for fit and comfort. I had nothing extra with me, and I mean nothing. I was only wearing jeans and sneakers. I had absolutely no food or water, but I'd had a few sips of water from the stream I was following. I was thirsty and didn't like doing it, since I didn't have a way to purify the water, but I had no choice.

*Maybe I'll get in trouble when I get back if I tell them I sipped the water,* I thought. *I know I'm not supposed to drink it unless it's purified. No, I have to tell them. They need to know. What if I get sick?*

As it grew darker, I crawled into my sleeping hole and pulled all the dirt and leaves I could find on top of me. Later, I discovered the temperature had dropped to 31 degrees, but I slept as well as you can trying to survive with little gear or equipment. I'll admit I got a little cold, but not much and I was more worried about wild animals than the cold.

Earlier today I'd seen a moose cow and her calf. They can be very dangerous, so I'd carefully walked away from them and once out of their sight, I ran. While moose can be mean, the thought of a bear scared me more than anything else. I found out after I was rescued that there were bears in the area and my brother, uncles and cousins who searched for me heard two for sure and maybe three.

They suspected I'd not sleep, because of all the noise being made by the coyotes. I didn't hear anything and I didn't feel overly frightened either. The last thing I remember was seeing a big full moon, so there was some light around me, and being tired. I have no idea at what time, but I eventually fell asleep.

My sleep was not sound or really restful, because I kept waking, tossing and turning. The best thing that happened is I survived the night in weather below freezing and without seeing a single animal once in my "bed." I and my family are certain I had lots of angels around me.

*****

**Dawn Ropelato's story for Saturday morning, August 13, 2011**

By the lights of our vehicle, as we drove to meet my husband at Spirit Lake, I grew ill at seeing all the many trees and dense brush. My mind began to flood with negative thoughts, and while I fought them hard, they remained. My mind flashed back to his birth and how we'd almost lost him then.

It was during one of his blessings as a newborn he was told he didn't need to live, but he could if he wanted to stay on earth. The choice was left up to him and we all knew which decision he'd made. I remembered how a few weeks ago he'd been tempted and how I felt like we'd kept him with us to be tempted. I felt a lot of guilt for putting him through all of this. I wondered if this time our Heavenly Father was going to spare him of anymore of life's trials. I'd been praying that all would be alright, that my son would be found safe, but then I realized I had to accept what was meant to be. I knew then, come what may, I would always be grateful for the years I'd shared with my son.

I worked hard to put those negative thoughts away and found a spot in my heart that filled me with hope and truly believed he'd be found safe and sound. I knew, no, I didn't just think, but *knew* I'd hold him again. It wasn't until much later, I learned my husband had similar thoughts and also agreed to accept the Lords will.

"Are you handling this okay?" I was jarred back to the present by the voice of Natalie.

"I have my up and down moments."

We pulled into the camp site at about 5 am, and Larry was easy to spot, because he was right in front of the aid station. I ran to him, he pulled me into his arms, and as we hugged, we both broke down right there. I saw Natalie hugging Justin and it broke my heart.

He looked so exhausted and my heart went out for him and all he'd experienced since he'd arrived. I knew he was spent, because he was one to try his best to find our son.

I met his eyes and asked, "How do you really feel?"

He fell to pieces and that worried me, so we just held each other as tightly as we could and cried together. That moment made me realize exactly how deeply I loved him and my whole wonderful family.

More people began to gather and form, and the sun started up around 6 am. The meeting to organize everyone was to start at 7, so to say I was anxious would be a great understatement. It was then I noticed the crowd was larger than I thought and I even saw horses. The sight of so many people brought me comfort and I felt loved. Some of these people were friends and family, while others were complete strangers, but they all shared a common goal—find our son.

Promptly at 7 the search and rescue briefing started. I was amazed at how many more people were now on hand. I was greatly relieved and I felt their love, as well as concern about our child. A quote quickly formed in my very busy mind, "Every human is born with a good heart."

Teams were quickly formed at this meeting, areas to search were assigned, and then the search began. It was an awesome sight to see all those people, many mounted on horses, move into the woods in search of my son.

A group prayer was held at 4 am at our church, and many were here now to help in any way they could. Some brought supplies, food, water or other items they knew we'd need. There were even two ladies no one recognized, but I found out later they were from my crafting group. I'd joined the group to associate with other good ladies. I felt then, that people are just good.

\*\*\*\*\*

**Larry Ropelato's story for Saturday morning, August 13, 2011**

It was decided to move the command center about four miles south the night before, because it was closer to where they suspected Jared would come out of the woods. The search and rescue commander happened to be our friend, Ben Wolford, and he went over what was planned for Saturday. The search teams would deploy and move into the woods at 7 am, with each responsible for a one-mile square segment, with four to eight people per team. The horses would search at the bottom, while the dog teams would start at the scout camp. They would then work toward each other, combing the underbrush and trees as they moved. If Jared continued to move, they suspected he'd walk out at the bottom, where the horses were starting their search. Actually, I discovered later that my son had walked past where the horses started. Ben also told me that my eighty-year old father, my son Kevin, my brother Scott, and my three nephews, Marc, Dave, and Jeff had checked in and were searching for Jared. I was asked to find them and tell them not to search through the night. I did not locate them this night, but they have their own story to tell.

The night before my son, Braxton, showed up to help, all the way from Jackson Hole, where he'd been with a Young Adult Ward. He was numb and had been crying so much his eyes were red. He was joined by Justin's in-laws, with horses, so I took Braxton and we drove the roads, just in case Jared had made it this far down. We saw no sign of my son, so we returned for Justin, and drove to the command center for the night. Blankets were provided by President Christensen and his wife, and from Sarah.

All three of us tried to get some sleep, but sleep comes hard to people worried about a family member. I slept for about thirty minutes, checked the temperature and it was forty-three degrees. I got up and sat in my vehicle, watching the time go by slowly and the temperature drop hour by hour. I could hear both Justin and Braxton snoring, so I know they were able to sleep, but I doubt it was truly rest or deep sleep.

I began to feel guilty about all the comforts that surrounded me and denied Jared. I even gave thought to walking into the woods and spending the night as he was, dealing with the elements. My body was exhausted, while my mind was active. My thoughts jumped around in all directions, but I finally decided to start the truck and dry my socks. I knew I needed sleep, so I'd have the strength to put in a full day tomorrow. I then prayed, not intending to close my prayer, asking that my son be found safe and that he would be able to stay warm overnight.

Then, my mind shifted to worrying about what we would eventually find. Would my son be found alive or dead? What if he was discovered dead? I knew I could not do the funeral services for my own son, so I'd have President Malone perform them for us. I pleaded with the Lord that we would at least recover Jared's body, if he was not to live. I needed him found, dead or alive, so I could touch my son. Not having a body to touch and mourn over would be difficult to handle.

Finally, at some point late in the night, I felt sure we'd find his body, only I wasn't sure if he'd be found alive. I did feel that my Heavenly Father and I had reached an agreement.

I began to feel guilty each time I started the truck for ten to twelve minutes to warm up. Each time I ran the heater, I thought of my baby out in the forest, with nothing but the clothes he wore. I knew he was cold, but was he injured too?

I now think I understand the book of Enos, in the Book Of Mormons, much better. I used to wonder how a person could pray all day and night, then wrestle with God. I feel that night I prayed hard and long, and then wrestled with God. I wrestled to get answers, to partially clean up some past history, and to make covenants with him. To me, this was all a bit scary, because I fully understood what I was asking and how hard it would be to keep my part of my commitment. I will do this.

All night long horse trailers were arriving, one after the other. I was touched by all of these people coming to help and watched as they unloaded their animals and prepared for the next morning. I knew about half were friends, some were acquaintances, and others were not known to me at all. Near 5 am, Dawn arrived.

Near 6, just as the sun was coming up, I found out that President Malone and Brad Merrill had organized a 9 pm meeting at the church to discuss and plan when to come to assist in the search. I was informed that the meeting had between eighty and ninety people, and Lance Mead, our High Priest group leader, had offered a prayer. They'd discussed getting people with horses, those who could walk, and those who could assist by bringing food and supplies. They had a prayer at 4 am for all of those who were coming to help. President Malone took charge of this early morning meeting and Brother Jones said the prayer (This could have been President Jones or Dean Jones, I'm unsure.) Following this meeting, all who wanted to search could come to help. Some of the women could not come, so they handed out peanut butter sandwiches and water to those leaving. People helped in many different ways.

After everyone was sent searching for Jared, I was asked to remain behind, in the event he was found so I could greet him, but I just couldn't do that. I had to be looking for my son and there was no way I could sit and wait. I knew if he wasn't found, I would never forgive myself for not going out and looking for him. I was sent to the closest grid to the command post, so I could be notified quickly once he was found. We were given all day to search our one mile grid.

We all agreed to stay close, because the woods were dense, so we could see each other at all times. According to the map, we had streams, swamps, steep hills, valleys, and marsh land to cover. I saw countless squirrels as we started moving. After a short distance, I saw we were starting to drift apart. Braxton had drifted away and to my guess, he may have been forty to fifty yards away. I called out to him, but he didn't respond. This worried me.

I ran up a small hill, maybe twenty feet high and when I saw how close he was I grew concerned. If he didn't hear me this closely, how would Jared be able to hear the search teams?

We'd covered about a mile into the forest when the radio came alive, "Justin or Larry, are you there?"

"Yes." I replied.

"Jared has been found."

I met Justin's eyes and said, "Easy, because the last time was a false alarm, remember?"

He nodded, but then said, "That's Ryan's voice."

"Yes, yes it is, so it must be true."

We moved to a higher area where reception was better and then contacted Ryan.

Justin took the radio and asked, "Where is Jared now?"

"He is here, at the command center."

"How is he doing?"

"His mother has him, but it's Jared."

I grew worried, because I didn't know if my son was alive or not. I'd known deep inside we'd find him, but what condition was he in?

We, Braxton and I, ran back to the road. Mike Jones was driving by at the exact time we neared, so he stopped and took me to the command center, while Braxton was dropped off at our truck. At the command center there were people milling all around and I didn't see Jared. I looked for him, but didn't see him. As I walked toward the command center, people moved out of my way as I walked. My dad, using his cane, was trying to get to the command center too, but I moved right on past him.

**Dawn Ropelato's story for Saturday morning, August 13, 2011**

I watched the search dogs going out to look for my son and grew worried, because Jared is afraid of dogs he doesn't know. I kind of hoped a dog would find him, so it might change his feelings about them. As I look back, I'm glad it wasn't a dog, because he had experienced enough over his long and slow night.

Some guys who were camping decided to try to help and they joined the search. They were driving their four-wheelers side by side as they looked. One of them felt they needed to look closer at an area they'd just passed, so back they went. As they drove, they yelled Jared's name.

Jared heard them, stood and began yelling back as he waved his arms. The young men heard him. Jared was on the other side of a canal or river; I'm not sure what it really was, but it had to do with water. They helped him across, fed him a light snack, and some water. I later heard them say he drank like a camel. They then gave him their hoodies to wear as they called in to report he'd been found. This was near 8:30 or 8:45 am.

I was near the command center, hugging and thanking people for coming, and watching others check in to search for my son, when Lisa Chandler called out to me. She was in their truck and she said, "Listen!" She held a walkie-talkie out the window.

When I neared, I heard Jared's name. I was hoping it was true, but wouldn't believe it until it had been confirmed.

Ryan, Lisa's husband said, "I've heard it four times."

I had so much worry, hope and fear bottled up inside of me, that I just broke down completely and started crying. I began to shake and my crying was not quiet, but my emotions flooded me and I had to get it out.

Then I heard someone yell, "There he is!"

I glanced in the direction folks were looking and he really was there! He was wearing an orange hoodie and looked so tired.

I ran to him and we embraced, both of us breaking into tears. I was so relieved and happy my baby had been found alive! During the years of my life, I've been happy many times, filled with joy, but having Jared safe in my arms filled me with absolute joy of the kind that cannot be explained, only felt.

We took him to the aid station and Sarah Wolford, a friend of mine, checked his vitals and made sure he was okay. He was soaked, from crossing the water, I think, but no signs of hypothermia were found. He had no clothes here, because they were with the search dogs. We had him undress and wrap up in a blanket.

"How is he?" I asked Sarah.

She smiled and said, "Perfect."

A little later, when Shirley came in to get a hug, Jared wouldn't let her go.

"Is there something I can do for you, Jared?" she asked.

"I want my dad."

I knew his dad was out looking for him and he was close. He was about a mile deep in the woods when he got our message that Jared had been found. He and Braxton ran to the road and met a car which brought them to the command center. I do not think running into the car was coincidence, but God had a hand in it.

I heard that Kevin, Scott, Dave, and Marc had searched all night. Marc and Kevin heard a few bears growling in the darkness and they weren't far away. I'm so glad Jared didn't hear them or he would have been terrified the whole night.

I loved seeing everyone hug Jared and it gave me such inner peace. From the smile on his face, he loved it as well.

Finally, he dressed in some of Trichelle's sweat pants. He then went out and shook hands with those around and thanked each one. A lot of hugs took place and love was expressed, which made me so proud of him.

I was told 306 volunteers had checked in this morning to look for my son. I looked around and knew there were even more that were waiting to check in, so the real number may never be known. Many of those people did not know a single member of my family, yet they were there to find my son.

\*\*\*\*\*

### Larry Ropelato's story for Saturday morning, August 13, 2011

I entered the command center and immediately saw my son. He looked exhausted, but happy.

The first thing I said to him was, "You did everything correctly."

We hugged, and then we cried.

Someone then said he'd done everything properly to survive the night and his efforts to stay warm were the best he could have done under the circumstances. I was relieved and proud of Jared.

I then let Gramps in and as they hugged and talked, I went out to speak to all the people that found my son. There were so many and I realized I couldn't thank them individually, so I yelled, "Can I have your attention!"

When it grew quiet, I said, "Thank you, I love you. I . . . I don't know what else to say."

My brother, Brent, shouted, "Enough has been said."

I spent the next hour mingling with folks and feeling the love from this group of people who'd volunteered their horses, machines, and time to look for our boy. What I needed and wanted most was to go home, but first the scouts had to see Jared was okay and safe.

When we met the scouts, it was heartwarming to see them run to Jared and hug him. Parents of the scouts had brought food for the boys, so they shared it with us. It was a reunion that I'm sure all involved will never forget. I, and I'm sure Jared, was glad when it was finally time to go home.

# PART 3

## Home at last

We arrived home to news reporters, neighbors, and friends. Our road was lined with yellow ribbons and balloons. Posters and gifts covered our garage and courtyard wall. Then candy grams and dinner were brought and the love continued and does to this day. It was good to talk with the reporters and have a good story to tell, with a happy ending.

Early Monday morning we were picked up at 3 am and taken to Salt Lake City, where we were interviewed by national news. We spoke with Good Morning America, the Today Show, and Fox.

See, on our way home, after Jared's rescue, I'd been contacted by Good Morning America, then the Today Show. I sent a message to Good Morning America and informed them that another show was also interviewing us. They were willing to share this story and weren't worried about it being told exclusively for them. When Fox called, they said they'd work it out with the others and did, too. The media organized it well, so it was easy for us.

Once at home after the interviews, ABC called and wanted to come on Tuesday, the next day, and do one last interview. I thought Jared was sick of all the cameras and interviews, so I told them Jared was exhausted and done.

"What about you? Can we interview you?"

I thought of Larry and replied, "I think you should talk with my husband, if you want an interview."

I felt Larry should do the interview because they hadn't heard much from him, since I was the one at home most of the time and available. I honestly felt an interview with him would be frosting on the cake and make everything associated with Jared's rescue complete.

The day they arrived, they kept the questions directed at Larry and I. I was glad because Jared really didn't want to be there and knew he was tired of all the publicity.

Jared was finally asked, "How does it feel, Jared, to be home now?"

"Good." was his fast reply.

After this interview the phones grew quieter, our lives returned to normal, and the pressures of the media disappeared. I took a nap and later, Jared and Kimleighel started fighting again. I smiled and thought, We're back to normal and guess what? I like our normal.

## Some of the Blessings Witnessed by Larry Ropelato

There is a family in our ward, no names mentioned, that was offended almost a year ago and they have repeatedly refused to return to our ward. The last time I spoke with them in my office, he'd stormed out and she left shortly after. I hadn't talked to either of them since. I sent them a letter, hoping to make things better and even dropped off root beer floats one night, but I felt as long as I remained Bishop, they would never come to church or talk to me again. While they have been attending another ward, their son cannot advance in the priesthood and they, the parents, cannot renew their temple recommends. They must do this is in our ward only. It was Friday night, as I was unable to sleep, I did some praying and thinking, that the thought came to me that this family would show up to search for Jared. Then I thought, *Yeah, right.*

Early the next morning, this family arrived. They both approached me and the mother gave me a hug, followed by the father.

As the father hugged me, I felt it was a tight and meaningful hug, he said, "We'll find your son."

"Thank you for coming." I said and meant it.

Suddenly, it was as if nothing had ever happened in the past.

After Jared was found, they participated in our group of friends as we talked. The next morning, in PEC, I asked the elders quorum President Carlos Baldwin, to call and invite them to church today and he did. They came to Sacrament meeting. After, I ran into them in the hall and thanked them for coming. They informed me they'd like to continue coming and they would like their son to receive the priesthood. So, I will meet with their son on Thursday to interview him and we'll ordain him to the office of a teacher on Sunday. This taught me a great deal about the Celestial Kingdom and how we all have differences in our lives, but when it really counts, we overlook our past differences and love each other. We join to serve our Father in Heaven the way He has taught us through his son, Jesus Christ. I feel this miracle happened because Jared got lost, or may I say, led away by the Holy Ghost. This miracle really happened in my life, so never give up on anyone.

About three months before all of this happened with Jared, I started riding my bike to work, which is nine miles. When I first started, it almost killed me, but after a couple of weeks, I was in really good shape. I think if not in such good shape for my age of 52, I could have had a heart attack while searching for my son. I am thankful the Lord prepared me for the ordeal physically.

After Jared was rescued, I asked him how, exactly, did he build his lean-to and bed. He said he remembered this from when he was working for his survival merit badge. He gathered some branches, small limbs, and then dug in the soil with his hands. Then he would lay in the hole to make sure he had the size and kept digging until it felt comfortable. He had to check the size about three times, but finally knew he'd fit. He sat up in the hole, covered his legs and lower body first with dirt and leaves. He covered the dirt and leaves with the branches, so they were on top of him. He laid down flat and covered the rest of his body up to his neck the same way. He then pushed his arm inside his bed as best as he could. We were very proud of him and what the scout leaders taught him.

My son shared some of his thoughts with me of that long night he spent alone. He kept hoping Ronnie would find him and that he'd not run into any bears.

"Did you hear any squirrels or the trees blowing in the wind." I asked.

"No, I did not hear anything but the noise of the helicopters flying over."

I know there had to be guardian angels assigned to him that night, on the perimeter of his small cold camp that kept all the noises, animals, and wind out of his sight and hearing. I think some sisters were also there to keep him warm. I find it interesting that the only noise he heard was the helicopters flying by as they searched for him. While he says he didn't get much sleep, Jared is a sound sleeper, so I suspect he probably did okay when he rested.

Our best guess is there were over 200 people looking for Jared the day he was found. Since he was found, we've heard that many more were on their way there, heard he'd been found, and then returned home. Others were getting ready to come, waiting for a ride or for another person to go with them, when my son was found. There is no question in my mind that if he'd not been found by early afternoon, well over 500 people would have been there by then.

One of the hardest things I had to do once I left Jared and went outside to speak with all the folds was to talk with Mr. Bardsley, who lost his son in the same area seven years ago. His son has never been found. He had Jared's path all mapped out and I was quite impressed. I asked him a few questions and then realized he's still searching for his son, seven years later.

I looked him in the eyes and my mind filled with all sorts of thoughts, but why did I get my son back and he didn't?

I was still looking in his eyes when I said, "I'm sorry." We then embraced and nothing more was needed to be said. However, I said, "Thank you for all you have done."

He's an expert on the area with all the GPS coordinates marked on maps and that is what the search and rescue folks used to assign search areas to our teams. I feel it was a great blessing that he had all that information on hand, and since his son was lost, he's helped find two others.

One important lesson I learned is if you make a mistake in the woods while walking is to make the best of your second decision. Jared did this. We all make bad mistakes, each of us, and the important thing to do is make the best of it and make a second choice that is smarter. After we make a wrong choice, it's important we remember that the Holy Ghost can still be with us and direct us to do what is right. I feel we're also teaching boys a double standard about what to do if they become lost. We tell them to stay in one spot, then we also tell them to do what needs to be done if you get lost. Jared chose to do what needs to be done and he followed it through with perfection.

Jared got tired of all the reporters and I did as well. One that I disliked the most was a local station that edited and rewrote what I said to the point it made it look as if I was mad at the scout leaders and this was not true. I felt their reporting made it look like the real reason Jared got lost was negligence on the part of the leaders and that's just not true either. I will never deal with them again. All other stations did an excellent job of reporting the story accurately.

Our friends, the Cox family, showed up on Saturday morning, and they were so emotional that I couldn't say anything.

Lynette Cox, sitting in the middle, looked at her daughter and said, "Get out, so I can give him a hug." Then, Naline got there and gave me a hug and we all started crying. I found out later that Lynette had bought all her kids 72 hour survival kits for Christmas and had pulled them from storage, thinking we might need them. Thank heavens that we didn't have to use them.

My good friend, Bruce, is a stake President in charge of 3 stakes, and they had a service project on Saturday morning. After they started the project, he asked everyone to say a prayer for Jared, first thing. Many told Bruce later that they'd already been praying for this little boy, ever since they'd heard about him being lost. Bruce and his friends had horses ready, so as soon as the project was over, they were going to look for Jared.

Ken Turner, with his boys and father, were in the Uintah's and were going to stay until Saturday, but he felt impressed to return home on Friday, right after they'd heard about Jared. They loaded up the horses, came to look for my son, and his father said, "Now you know why you felt impressed to come home."

Dean Hill, another friend of mine, told me when he heard about Jared, he went to get his horses ready.

His wife came out and said, "You can't go, because you just had a hip replaced and you're not to ride a horse for two more months."

I'm glad he listened to his wife, but it's interesting how he only thought of this lost child and not himself.

Grandma Lowe called her grandsons, told them Jared was lost, and they should gather up horses and friends to look for Jared. She volunteered to pay for their gas and food. This was her way of helping and I'm guessing she's near 90 years young. People all helped in different ways.

On August the 16th, I was at work and exhausted. All the events, lack of sleep and excitement had worn me out. I was talking on the phone and noticed my niece, Shay Coy, standing by the soft-drink machine. I noticed she didn't approach me, so I got off the phone and went to her.

She started crying and hugged me as she said, "I just have to hug someone from our family."

Feeling badly, because she'd not been able to go look for Jared as it was too far from her, she'd stopped by the shop. She hugged me, and I didn't think she was ever going to let go.

She said, "I can't wait for mom to get back in town, so I can go to Hooper and visit Jared. I want to hug him and Dawn both."

She loves our family and shows it, too.

She then shared an experience with me. She said, "I've never really fasted in my life, but felt the urge last Thursday, but didn't act on it. I did think about it all day and the thought kept coming back to me. Friday morning, when I woke up, I had an urge to fast again. After I started fasting, I heard about Jared and was happy I could fast for him and our family."

I reminded her that she followed the promptings of the Holy Ghost, without knowing why.

Then she realized God really did speak to her, she'd listened, and suddenly broke into tears again. We discussed what happened to Jared, our family, and the experiences, so we ended up crying again. A few minutes later, we were laughing. She gave me energy to make it through the rest of the day. I keep hearing of experiences like hers and I'm amazed at how many people Jared and his survival situation affected in this way.

On Sunday morning, August 14th, 2011, Durk Bailey, our neighbor came over to see Jared and presented him with a gold medal he'd won just months ago in the Senior Olympics. My son wore it around his neck, even to church, until he went to pass the sacrament. Our neighbors have been so kind and loving to Jared, and all of us actually. I easily reached the conclusion we have the best neighbors.

**Folks that comforted Dawn Ropelato**

There were many that came to comfort me: Naline Lee, Paul and Debbie Widdison, Bradi Widdison, La Verna Gray and her girls, Keri and Sabrina, Cindy Pendleton, President Malone and Kathy, Judy and Scott Nauta, Suzie Arave, Shirley Stokes, Tami and Shelby Ropelato, Jen Simpson, and her aunt Bonnie Norris, Tyler and Melanie Ropelato, and also Natalie Ropelato. I deeply appreciate the loving support I received from each of them. It's possible I've left a name or perhaps more than one name out, but it is not intentional, and God knows all who brought me comfort and support. My deepest apologies if your name is not listed.

**Lessons from our experience by Dawn Ropelato:**

1. God hears and answers prayers and he loves us and knows us.

2. People care about others, even though they don't know them personally.

3. We get promptings that prepare us for things to come.

4. We need each other; leaders taught and prepared Jared, we all teach each other.

5. We need to listen more, to each other and the spirit. Jared heard others calling him the first day, but they were so anxious they didn't stop to listen for his reply, we all do that some times.

6. Lastly, we all make wrong choices in our lives every now and then, but we can still get back on the path, and return to safety, with the help of our Lord and friends.

I felt like Abraham having to sacrifice my son, and even though I was willing, I didn't have to give him up. That thought came to me around 4:30 am on the drive to where he'd been lost.

I also understand the story of Naomi and her mother-in-law, and how she stayed by her side. Natalie was by my side through all of this. It meant a lot to me. Jared's experience was much more than a scout taking the wrong path and getting lost; to us, it was so much more.

## Author's final comments

As I stated at the beginning of this book, Jared is a very survival savvy young man and in the time he was missing, death could have easily visited him in the form of a mishap, hypothermia, or a dozen other dangers. Thanks to the efforts of others, both physically and in prayer, Jared was saved. I know all survivors pray, from all that I've ever read about or talked with about their experiences.

As a survival professional, the only thing he made a poor decision in was by not stopping and waiting, but it's very typical for a child. Keep in mind, this was no adult, but an eleven year old boy and once he made the poor decision, he quickly adjusted and survived, just as he'd been taught. It's easy for armchair survival experts to point out this or that, but it's a little harder when you're in the field, tired, hungry and scared.

Jared, God must have a special life selected for you with many challenges, so face each one as you did your survival situation and you'll do fine. I'm proud of you, young man.

# GLOSSARY

**Please note,** this glossary is in no way complete and Search and Rescue uses countless terms, as well as acronyms, when doing business. Some smaller civilian and military teams may have a language almost to itself they use on a daily basis. However, with that said, here are some of the most common ones. If written using the field language, few readers would be able to follow the story line, so I've smoothed it out a bit.

**360:** When an aircraft flies 360 degrees, or a circle. Often done when waiting for further instructions, to burn fuel on purpose, or preparing and waiting to land.

**Abort:** To cancel or call off the flight of an aircraft

**AC:** Aircraft Commander, the pilot

**AO:** Area of operations

**ATV:** All Terrain Vehicle, used most often by hunters and guides, but also used by Search and Rescue personnel. Gas powered and excellent small vehicles for rough country. Older ones have three wheels, but new ones have four.

**Assistant Team Leader**: The number two man in charge of a team of military or civilian men.

**Band-aid:** Often a radio call sign for a medic

**BDU**: Camouflage field uniform used by military personnel

**Bingo on fuel:** Running out or low on aircraft fuel.

**Bird:** Helicopters or any type of aircraft

**Blood trail:** A trail of blood left by a person who has been injured

**Body bag:** Plastic or rubber bag used to transport dead bodies from crash sites

**Bush:** Military term for the field (woods, mountains, and so on)

**CAP:** Civil Air Patrol, a very helpful group of civilian aircraft that assist in stateside rescues and recovery.

**Chinook:** CH-47 cargo helicopter

**Chopper:** A slang name for a helicopter

**Clock Positions:** 12 O'clock would be straight ahead, while 6 would be directly behind you. Each number on a watch can be related to a position for the aircraft pilot or a team on the ground.

**Command Center:** The centralized location for all commanders, leaders and those managing the search and rescue in the civil world. In the military, often the command post is where these men and women meet to make decisions.

**Copy:** I understand, hear you, know what you mean, etc...an acknowledgment of understanding. Or it may be a question, do you copy? Do you understand?

**Countdown:** Used by the survivor to indicate to a rescue aircraft when they fly overhead. Used mostly in areas with limited visibility and is an actual countdown starting with any number, but when the aircraft is overhead, the survivor says, "Overhead now!"

**CP:** Command Post

**Doc:** Medic, corpsman, or doctor

**D-ring:** A D-shaped metal snap link used to hold gear together and used in rappelling from choppers.

**Dust-off:** Medical evacuation helicopter

**EM:** Enlisted man

**ETA:** Estimated time of arrival

**ETD:** Estimated time of departure

**EMT:** Emergency Medical Technician

**Evac:** See Medivac

**Expectant:** Casualties who are expected to die

**Fast Movers:** Jet aircraft.

**Field Surgical Kit:** Kit carried by medics in the field for small surgery and suturing.

**Five by five:** Used in radio communications to indicate the radio is working and messages are heard loud and clear.

**Flaky:** To be in a state of mental disarray or disorganized

**Flare, MK-13:** A flare that has both a day and night end. The night end generates a very bright light that was visible for a long distance, while the day end gives off a thick cloud of bright orange smoke; see smoke grenade.

**Flare, Pen-gun:** Illumination projectile; hand-fired

**Grids:** Maps are broken into numbered thousand-meter squares and each is a grid.

**HQ:** Headquarters

**Horn:** Radio or Telephone

**Huey:** Nickname for UH-1 helicopters

**Hump:** Military term: walk carrying a rucksack in the field.

**IG:** Inspector General

**Immersion foot:** Condition resulting from feet being submerged in water or being wet for a prolonged period of time, causing cracking and bleeding. Easily prevented by keeping the feet dry and using clean socks.

**Insert:** To be deployed into a tactical area, usually by helicopter

**K-bar:** A military combat knife

**Klick:** Kilometer

**Litters:** Stretchers to carry wounded

**LT:** Lieutenant

**LZ**: Landing zone. Usually a small clearing secured temporarily for the landing of resupply helicopters

or Medivac's.

**Medevac:** Medical evacuation helicopter used in combat areas and in peacetime

**Meals Ready to Eat (MRE):** Military meals. Small sealed pouches that contains an entrée and side dish, along with a dessert and other small food items. They do not require heating but taste better hot. Lightweight with a high calorie count.

**MIA:** Missing in action. Meaning lost or missing as a result of combat with an enemy force.

**Mike(s):** Minute or minutes

**NCO**: Noncommissioned officer.

**Number one:** The best of anything

**Number ten:** The worst or no good.

**OD:** Olive drab is a color of green used by the military

**Over:** Means the communication is completed, so the other person on the radio can talk next.

**Over and Out:** Means the communication is completed and the speaker is finished speaking. End of conversation.

**Out:** See Over and Out above.

**Forest Penetrator**: A device lowered by a wench from a chopper to the ground to pick up survivors. It has a safety strap, three folding seats, and can be used in thick forests or in limited visibility situations.

**PJ: (Poppa Juliet)** Pararescueman, which used to be called Para-Jumpers. A highly trained individual who works as a rescue specialist and medic. Trained for rescue and recovery and called P.J.'s.

**Point:** The forward most man on a military patrol

**Poncho liner:** Nylon insert to the military rain poncho, used as a blanket frequently.

**Pop smoke:** To ignite a smoke grenade to signal a rescue aircraft or show wind direction.

**PRC-25:** Portable Radio Communications, Model 25. A back-packed FM receiver-transmitter used for short-distance communications. The range of the radio is 5-10 kilometers, depending on the weather, unless attached to a special, non-portable antenna which could extend the range to 20-30 kilometers

**PRC-90**: Small portable hand-held survival radio, usually carried in a survival vest or packed in a survival kit for aircrew members.

Range is generally line of site and very poor in mountainous terrain.

**Rescue Center:** Where all the planning, organization and moves are planned and directed. The head of the whole rescue operation. They can have other names, but one central spot does all the coordination of the rescue.

**Roger:** Correct or right. Used to answer questions.

**RTO:** Radio telephone operator.

**Ruck / rucksack:** Term used for a backpack issued to military personnel.

**Saddle up**: Put a pack on and get ready to move out

**Slack man:** The second man back from the point, on a military patrol, directly behind the point man, or first man.

**Smoke grenade:** A grenade that releases brightly colored smoke. Used for signaling Medivac and rescue choppers. Used mostly by other services and not as much by the United States Air Force. Air Force personnel would use an MK-13 smoke signal, with bright orange smoke.

**SOP:** Standard Operating Procedure or the written way things are done.

**Stokes litter:** A basket looking device, similar to a stretcher that is lowered by wench from a chopper to a survivor for pick up. Usually used when injured are discovered.

**Starlight scope or Night Vision Goggles:** A night scope, or goggles, used to intensify images at night by using reflected light from the moon, stars or any other source of light.

**SRU-21/P Survival Vest:** A mesh vest worn by aircrew members that contains survival gear to keep them alive and to assist in rescue. It has flares, radio, matches and much more for survival.

**Strobe Light**: Hand held strobe light for marking landing zones at night

**Team Leader:** The leader of a team of military or civilian men and women. He/she is in charge. In the military the team leader can be either an officer or NCO, depending on the mission.

**Thumbs up:** A visual communication, non verbal, that indicates all is well or okay. Also used to let the wench operator on a chopper know you're ready to be lifted aboard the aircraft.

**UH-1H:** a Huey helicopter and an old medivac workhorse.

**Visual:** I see it or have it visual.

**Wait One:** Wait a minute, or just a second. Used usually when the person on the radio has to contact someone else.

**Wood line:** A row of trees at the edge of a field

# ABOUT THE AUTHOR

Copyright 2013 by Melanie C. Benton

**W.R. Benton**, a pen name, is a retired U.S. military senior Non-commissioned Officer with over twenty-six years of active duty service. He grew up in the Missouri Ozark Mtns., where hunting, trapping, camping, and other outdoor activities were the norm. Additionally, he spent more than twelve years teaching survival and parachuting procedures to U.S. Air Force personnel as a Life Support instructor. Mister Benton has an Associate's Degree in Search and Rescue, Survival Operations, a Bachelors Degree in Occupational Safety and Health, and a Masters Degree in Psychology near completion.

Mister Benton is a member of the America Authors Association (AAA). You can visit W.R. Benton online http://www.wrbenton.net or his *War Paint* Site at http://www.warpaint.info.

And on Facebook ⓕ www.facebook.com/wrbenton01

*Alive and Alone*

*Available in paperback & for the Kindle at Amazon.com*

### A Story of Survival and faith...

On a trip to the Lake Clark area of the Alaskan bush, a sudden arctic weather system forces down the small plane of Dr. Jim Wade, and his son David. Both have survived the crash, but not unscathed. Food, fire and shelter are all a priority. Following the death of his father, now it is up to David to figure out what to do next, and how to survive, on a remote Alaskan mountain - in winter!

This is a fictional story of survival, resilience and of the spirit to live. It is both authentic and accurate, having been written by a former Air Force life support survival instructor.

**Young adult: For ages 12 and up**

## SIMPLE SURVIVAL

*Available in paperback & for the Kindle at Amazon.com,
Nook, Kobo and iBooks versions.*

*Read Gary's guide and you'll be ready for nearly anything...*

"Retired USAF Senior Master Sergeant and survivor expert Gary Benton has written
the best outdoor guide for families - bar none, that I have read! "Simple Survival - A
Family Outdoors Guide" is more than a book - it is an outdoor resource bible that
every family should have a copy of. This is one of those books that you should have
in your camping bag along with the tent and other equipment.

There is one chapter that deals with the greatest fears that all parents have - having your child get lost in the woods. This is a must read for parents. This information needs to be shared with all their children so they know what to do in the event
of getting lost or separated from their parents or the campsite. This is the kind of
information that you hope you never need to put into use.

— Bill McDonald - MWSA President

# Audiobooks by W.R. Benton

Available now at Audible.com and iTunes

Printed in Great Britain
by Amazon

40613868R00116